ELVIS
*⁂*and the
Gra*teful Dead*

**Center Point
Large Print**

Also by Peggy Webb
and available from Center Point Large Print:

Elvis and the Dearly Departed

ELVIS
and the
Grateful Dead

Peggy Webb

CENTER POINT PUBLISHING
THORNDIKE, MAINE

This Center Point Large Print edition
is published in the year 2010 by arrangement with
Kensington Publishing Corp.

The text of this Large Print edition is unabridged.
In other aspects, this book may vary
from the original edition.
Printed in the United States of America.
Set in 16-point Times New Roman type.

ISBN: 978-1-60285-623-3

Library of Congress Cataloging-in-Publication Data

Webb, Peggy.
  Elvis and the grateful dead / Peggy Webb.
    p. cm.
  ISBN 978-1-60285-623-3 (library binding : alk. paper)
1. Beauty operators--Fiction. 2. Cousins--Fiction. 3. Basset hound--Fiction.
  4. Festivals--Fiction. 5. Elvis Presley impersonators--Crimes against--Fiction.
  6. Murder--Investigation--Fiction. 7. Tupelo (Miss.)--Fiction. 8. Large type books.
  I. Title.

PS3573.E1985E59 2010
813'.54--dc22

2009038306

*For my dream team, agent Kelly Harms
and editor John Scognamiglio,
with love and deepest gratitude
for giving me the freedom to write with wings.*

ELVIS
and the
Grateful Dead

Elvis' Opinion #1 on Impersonators, the Valentine Family, and Fried Pigskins

If you ask me, all these impersonators running around Tupelo in sequined jumpsuits could use remedial voice lessons. Nobody can hold a candle to the King. That would be me, though these days I could pass through a crowd unnoticed if it weren't for my pink bow tie. I also wanted to wear my black pompadour to the Elvis Festival, but Callie (my human mom) said basset hounds look silly in toupees.

What does she know? Don't get me wrong. She's the best human mom a dog could have, but she can't even keep her own life straight, much less mine. If she'd seek my sage advice, I'd tell her to stop trying to take care of the world (and that includes picking up stray dogs and cats as well as loaning money to everybody with a sob story who walks into her beauty shop). Mostly, though, I'd tell her to drop divorce proceedings.

If any two people belong together, it's Callie and Jack (my human daddy). She says they split over his Harley Screamin' Eagle, but I know better. They split because she wants a family and he's worried about having children and then getting shot and leaving them fatherless.

Of course, he's never told Callie the truth because he's never even told her about his real

9

profession—and if I told you, I'd have to kill you. Suffice it to say, Jack Jones makes Rambo look timid.

Callie and Jack are at an impasse and "All Shook Up." At the rate things are going, it looks like I'll be punted between them for the next three years. Like a pigskin.

Speaking of which, I think I'll mosey on over to the refreshment booth and see what's cooking. Fried pigskins, for one thing. Lovie's in charge. She shares my opinion that the body ought to be primed with sugar and fat. (Spirits, too, which she uses generously in her catering business recipes, though Callie would die if she knew her cousin sometimes slips me a little of her Jack Daniel's apple pie.)

Take it from me, Lovie and I know a thing or two. She's a hundred-and-ninety-pound bomb-shell with plenty of curves to hold on to; and in spite of my slightly mismatched ears and my portly figure, I'm a suave dog and a force to be reckoned with. We've both had more lovers than I've had hit records. But ever since Ann-Margret batted her French poodle eyes at me and Rocky Malone blew into Lovie's life during what the Valentine family now refers to as the Bubbles Caper, we've both been testing the waters of love everlasting.

Frankly, if it weren't for the example set by Ruby Nell (Callie's mama) and Charlie (Lovie's

Daddy) I'd be howling "Rock-a-Hula Baby" instead of "Wear My Ring Around Your Neck." Both of them had great marriages and still worship the quicksand their immortal beloveds walked on. (Even a Rock 'N' Roll King knows his Beethoven.)

If you ask me (which nobody does around here), Ruby Nell and Charlie would benefit from a good dose of "Love Me Tender" with somebody who is not six feet under. In fact, I might help her find a savvy senior gentleman who appreciates a woman who walks on the wild side so she'll stay out of Callie's hair (and her pocketbook).

While I'm at it, I might find Charlie a smart, witty woman who still pays homage to her libido. A nice romance could be the key to unlock the passion he hides under the facade of godfather to the entire Valentine family.

If I could be like Ruby Nell and Charlie in my next life, I wouldn't mind coming back as a human. Not that there's anything wrong with being a dog. Put a bassett hound in the White House and he'd have this country straightened out before you could say *pass the Pup-Peroni.*

Hot on the scent of grease, I detour by the T-shirt booth for a whole lotta lovin' from Charlie and Ruby Nell, then nose around the festival so everybody can get a gander at the real King. Listen, I may be a basset hound, but I know what I know:

11

(1) impersonators singing flat notes and wearing hair gel you can smell a mile ought to be banned from wearing sequined jumpsuits, and (2) life's better with a lot of petting and a hefty portion of fried pigskins.

Chapter 1

Hair Gel, Flat Notes, and the Rockabilly Corpse

Here comes Elvis looking so cute I don't have the heart to chastise him for slipping his leash. "There you are, boy." I secure his leash and tighten the collar a notch, then give him some extra petting so he won't get miffed.

Not many people can say they're where they are because of a dog. But let me tell you, if it weren't for Elvis I'd be a free woman sitting on a beach somewhere with a man who has daddy potential. By the time I settle my dog-custody battle with Jack Jones, my eggs are going to be on life support.

But I'm not about to give up Elvis, even if he is the reason I'm legally tied to a man who went out to buy a baby cradle and came back with a Harley. If Jack thinks he can deprive me of progeny and have my dog, too, he has another *think* coming. I'd as soon give up Mama.

Elvis is part of my family. And family is the reason I'm dispensing hair gel and pompadours from a tent in a corner of the blocked-off section of downtown Tupelo instead of shoring up my finances at Hair.Net (my little beauty shop in Mooreville, population six hundred and fifty— and a half since Fayrene's niece got pregnant).

13

Uncle Charlie is on the Elvis Festival Committee. When he said *we should all do our civic duty and help out with this year's festival,* it might as well have been an edict from God. Not only does Uncle Charlie own and manage the most popular funeral home in northeast Mississippi (Eternal Rest), but he manages to keep the entire Valentine family sane (barely) and out of trouble (mostly). We think he walks on water.

As for my dog, Elvis considers it his birthright to be on display at the annual Elvis Festival. When I mentioned I might leave him home so he could use the doggie door to get inside and stay cool, he chewed the laces off my Reeboks, then deliberately heisted his leg on my prize petunias.

He's sporting his pink bow tie. Personally, I can see why my dog thinks he's Mississippi's most famous son reincarnated. The way he's swaggering while Brian Watson belts out "Don't Be Cruel," you can almost see the swivel-hipped King himself.

Brian has a hitch in his swivel. Elvis trots to the tent opening and shoots him a disdainful look before ambling over to sit at my feet. I bend down to scratch his ears.

"Are you about ready for the tour of the Birthplace, boy? Promise you won't go running off again." I take his grin as a *yes.* I swear my dog looks human when he smiles.

Brian is the last of today's competitors vying for

tribute artist fame. As soon as the new *American Idol* winner takes the stage, Lovie and I will escort the impersonators on a tour of the famous Birthplace in east Tupelo.

I'm getting ready to shut down my on-site beauty salon when Lovie strolls in, hands me a glass of iced peach tea, and plops in front of the makeup mirror.

"If Brian's notes get any flatter, I may have to join Aunt Ruby Nell in a five o'clock toddy."

Mama always says *a little libation is good for the spirit,* and I guess she's right because she's one of the liveliest spirits I know.

"Pretty me up, Callie. Rocky's going to call."

"He can't see you over the telephone."

"If I feel sexy, I talk sexy. Work your magic."

I grab a comb and set to work.

Rocky Malone is her current heartthrob, and from the looks of things, her last. Thanks to the teddy-bear charm of the man we thought wanted to kill us over the Bubbles Malone caper, Lovie's likely to marry and end up in Las Vegas. Then what will I do?

I know, *I know.* This sounds selfish. But Lovie's not only my first cousin, she's also my best friend, my confidant, and my cohort in crime. (Thank goodness, I'm not a criminal, but if you had been with us when we tried to steal a corpse and haul it across the desert in ninety-degree heat, you'd know what I'm talking about.)

I put the finishing touch on Lovie's flaming red mane. "What's Mama doing with a five o'clock toddy? It's only three."

"When has reason ever applied to Aunt Ruby Nell? She said she wanted to be ready for your party tonight."

Mama's farm in Mooreville is only a fifteen-minute drive from Tupelo and I know it doesn't take her four hours to get ready for a party. Something else is afoot. I just hope it doesn't involve Fayrene's back room at Gas, Grits, and Guts (Mooreville's one and only convenience store) and that jar of quarters Fayrene keeps on the table.

For the Coke machine, is what Mama always says, but don't let my cute shoes fool you; I'm nobody's dummy. I've seen the deck of cards Fayrene keeps stashed behind the Sweet N Low.

I don't have time to worry about such things because Jack Jones comes strolling in looking like something you'd want to eat with a spoon. I'm learning to resist. With my almost-ex, you always bite off more than you can chew.

"I was just passing through and thought I'd take Elvis off your hands."

Passing through, my foot. Jack was spying. Ever since we separated I can't go to the grocery store without discovering him lurking behind the Charmin. And believe me, it's not toilet tissue he's planning to squeeze.

"Whatever happened to hello?"

Major mistake. Jack stalks across the tent, pulls me hard against his chest, and kisses me senseless. Or at least, addled.

"Hello, Callie." He winks at Lovie.

I try to act like I don't want to take him to Reed's Department Store and pick out Egyptian cotton sheets and new dishes, but with my cheeks on fire that's hard to do.

"If you'll care to remember, Elvis has a particular love of this festival. Why don't you do us both a favor and get lost in a Brazilian jungle?"

"Then who would keep your cute buns out of trouble?"

"I would. That's who."

He walks out, *laughing*. I want to bop him with my blow-dryer.

"Of all the nerve. I ought to . . . to *date*."

"Why don't you?" Lovie's not asking a question; she's issuing a challenge.

"Because . . ." Jack still makes me want to cook gingerbread, wear his favorite perfume, and wash his socks. And that's the least of it. If I don't get him out of my head soon, I might as well sign up to announce my cracked-to-pieces love life on the Dr. Phil show. "Maybe I *will* date."

"Good." Lovie stands up and hugs me. "Let's get this tour over with so I can go home and get a chocolate fix. Beulah Jane Ball is driving me crazy."

"Shush, Lovie. Here she comes."

In her daisy print dress and sturdy support stockings, Beulah Jane looks like a little grandmother who's too timid to share her cookie recipe. Her appearance is misleading to say the least. She could run China. As president of the local Elvis Presley fan club, she's not only lording over the refreshment booth—which everybody knows is managed by Lovie—but also trying to run the whole show.

"Callie, Lovie, hurry along now. The tour bus is waiting." Beulah Jane shoos us out of the tent with a cardboard fan on a stick featuring the King as a shy, skinny boy on the cusp of fame. When she sees Elvis, she gives a little mock horror screech. "That *dog's* not coming, is he?"

"Yes. He's with me." I grab Elvis and board the bus behind Lovie. Furthermore, we take a front seat. Uncle Charlie put us in charge of this tour, and I'm not about to let Beulah Jane take over.

She clambers in behind us, along with the club's other top-ranking officers, Tewanda Hardy and Clytee Estes. Tewanda pauses besides us, pats her tight curls, glares at Elvis over the top of her wire-rim glasses, and sniffs. "Lord have mercy. Gladys Presley would roll over in her grave."

I guess it's her tacky hairdo that makes Tewanda so mean. Whoever put that blue rinse on her gray hair and then wound it on little bitty perm rods ought to be shot.

Instead of passing along some styling advice, I mind my own business (a point of pride with me considering I run the kind of shop that makes my clients feel free to talk). Sitting back, I watch the impersonators board. The first is Brian Watson, a waiter at the Longhorn Steak House in Huntsville, Alabama, who looks the part but lacks the pipes. Next is Dick Gerard, a postman and local celebrity who rose to impersonator fame at the Tupelo Luncheon Civitan Club when he ate too much fried chicken and split the seat right out of his tight pink jumpsuit.

The third contest hopeful to board is a woman. From Australia, of all places. Elisha Stevens, though she prefers to be called Eli. Her black slick-backed hair is real. I know because I styled it. Her imitation of the King is on target, too. Only her sideburns and her southern accent are fake.

Behind her are the tribute artists from Japan and Italy, who both wanted to take me out to dinner. If Jack Jones keeps acting like the guardian from you-know-where, I might just say yes. To both of them.

Right now, though, I have a civic duty to perform. After the last contestant boards, Beulah Jane, Tewanda, and Clytee pass around cookies and peach tea. I tap the driver on the shoulder, and we set off down Main Street on the first leg of our Elvis pilgrimage.

Picking up the bus' microphone, I start my spiel.

"On the left you'll see Tupelo Hardware Store where Gladys took her son to buy a present for his tenth birthday. He wanted a bicycle, but she couldn't afford that. His second choice was a BB gun, but Gladys didn't believe in weapons, so Elvis Presley ended up with his first guitar."

When Beulah Jane pops up and says, "Tell the price," Lovie grabs the microphone and says, "She was getting to that."

Holy cow. If I don't get these two separated, we're going to make festival history. I can see the headlines now. *Fan Club President Beat to Death with Baseball Bat.* Lovie's weapon of choice.

Not that she could get it in her purse, but with Lovie, you never know. Her rainbow-colored peasant skirt is big enough to slipcover Texas. She might have the bat strapped to her leg.

To top it off, Elvis, who's nosing around scavenging for cookie crumbs, is eyeing Beulah Jane's Easy Spirits with wicked intent. I wouldn't be caught dead in those shoes, but I don't want my dog peeing on them. Whipping a Pup-Peroni stick out of my purse, I say, "Come here, boy."

Food always brings him running. With my dog safely stowed, I point out City Hall with its dancing water fountain, built on the old Mississippi/Alabama fairgrounds, which was the site of Elvis' famous 1956 homecoming concert.

"Elvis left Tupelo a thirteen-year-old kid from the wrong side of the tracks without much future and returned a recording star with a parade in his honor," I tell the busload of impersonators, who swivel to look at the old fairgrounds. "Every high school marching band played Elvis songs; the local merchants had Elvis displays in the window, and the Rex Plaza served up Love Me Tender Steak, Hound Dogs with Sauerkraut, Rock 'N' Roll Stew, and Oobie Doobie Cake with Tutti-Frutti Sauce."

Everybody swivels to look at the dancing waters. Even Bulah Jane is mollified, though her satisfaction would be short-lived if she knew Elvis was still *pointing* her shoes.

The minute we get to the Birthplace, I'm putting him on a leash . . . and buying chocolate to calm Lovie.

With impersonators swarming all over the gift shop, the museum, the chapel, and the shotgun house where the King was born, Lovie and I are sitting beside the fountain taking a breather and eating Hershey's bars.

"I know this is going straight to my hips." Lovie pats her ample thighs. "Fortunately Rocky likes his women round."

"I wish it would go to mine." I look like a swizzle stick. Especially beside Lovie. And especially since Jack left and my appetite went down the drain. All arms and coltish-looking legs and big brown eyes. Chest flat as a flitter.

Mama has the classy movie star looks of a past-her-prime Katharine Hepburn while Lovie has the glamour and lush beauty of Rita Hayworth. Even Uncle Charlie can still turn heads. At sixty-three, no less. But the good looks fairy passed me by. My two best features are my clear olive skin and my thick brown hair. Which, thanks to my expertise, always looks like it ought to be featured on the pages of *Glamour*.

Everybody has to have something to brag about, and I guess with me, it's my sleek, stylish hair.

Lovie's cell phone rings and when she sees the number pop up, she tells me, "Rocky."

I've never seen her like this—her blue eyes shining and her voice dreamy.

"Hey, baby." She never calls anybody *baby,* not even Elvis, whom she adores. This is a Lovie I don't even know.

I'm happy for her, really I am. But a little scared, too. As I leave the fountain and walk my dog toward the statue of a barefoot, teenaged Elvis wearing overalls and carrying his cherished guitar, I say a little prayer that my cousin, who has never, ever been in love, doesn't lose herself in this new territory.

I also say a little prayer for myself. Jack and I used to call each other pet names. The sound of his voice used to make me misty-eyed. (Sometimes it still does, but I'm not going there.) If I thought I'd never have that kind of love again, I'd chop off my hair and join a nunnery.

Of course, that's a little extreme, especially since I'd have to give up cute designer shoes. Maybe I'd just leave Mooreville and go somewhere exotic. Or at least, someplace where Jack is *not.*

Impersonators are lined up to get their pictures made with the bronze image of their icon, so I volunteer as cameraman. When they find out my dog is named Elvis, they invite him to be in the pictures.

Naturally he tries to steal the show. And I'll have to say he's succeeding. Next year maybe I'll have him a little sequined doggie jumpsuit made.

Elvis puts on his best smile—tongue lolling out, lower lips pulled back—till Beulah Jane walks by clapping her hands.

"Listen up, Elvises! It's time to load the bus! Chop, chop, everybody!"

As he makes a beeline for her bony ankle, I grab Elvis' leash. "Don't even think about it."

The impersonators nab cameras and bulging bags from the gift shop, then rush after Beulah Jane.

Lovie strolls up wearing a big grin. "What's the one-woman hostility committee up to now?"

"Herding the tribute artists to the bus."

Lovie consults her watch. "We have fifteen minutes. What's her hurry?"

"Never mind. Let her enjoy being in charge. Tell me about Rocky."

"He's coming to Tupelo."

"When?"

"In a few days. He's flying with a friend in a private plane."

"That's good news, Lovie."

"*Good,* my foot. You can hear my vagina shouting hallelujah all the way to the state line."

Now, *that's* the Lovie I know and adore. I link my arm through hers and we head to the bus.

Beulah Jane is standing up front, her lips moving as she counts heads.

"We seem to be one Elvis short," she tells me.

"Who's missing?" As I scan the crowd, it doesn't take me long to realize our missing impersonator is the waiter from Huntsville. "Has anybody seen Brian?"

Eli, the lone female artist, stands up at the back. "I saw him in the chapel about five minutes ago."

"Everybody stay put. Lovie and I will check."

Even if Brian is not in the chapel, he can't be far. The Birthplace is very small with all the buildings clustered in an area little more than a city block. Grabbing Elvis, we trudge across the parking lot, past the gift shop, and up the hill toward the small 'seventies-style chapel. I don't dare leave him unattended on the same bus with Beulah Jane.

"Listen, Lovie. Is that music?"

"If that's music, I'm a hot buttered biscuit."

Elvis, who obviously agrees with Lovie, heists his leg on a native hibiscus bush.

I recognize the flat tenor notes wafting from the

chapel. It's Brian, all right, playing the piano and wailing, "I once was lost but now am found . . ."

Suddenly there's a discordant crash and "Amazing Grace" comes to a halt. I have the sick feeling you'd get if you were standing on the deck of the *Titanic* and felt it tilting under your feet.

"Hurry." Grabbing Lovie's arm, I half drag her and Elvis up the last stretch and through the chapel doors. It's dim in here and it takes a minute for my eyes to adjust.

Then I see our missing impersonator—slumped over the keyboard of the upright piano.

"Brian!"

He doesn't answer, doesn't move. I call out again, but he's very, very still.

Elvis' hackles come up and he starts growling. Not a good sign.

I squeeze Lovie's arm, and she squeezes back.

"I don't like this, Callie."

Neither do I. But I didn't earn my reputation as the best hair and makeup artist in Mississippi by backing down from the hard stuff.

When I'm not making Mooreville's glitterati look glamorous at my little beauty parlor, I'm over at Uncle Charlie's fixing up the dead. You wouldn't think I'd be squeamish in a situation like this. But you'd be wrong. Under Uncle Charlie's vigilance, death is tamed, demystified, and even friendly. Beyond his watchful eye, anything could be waiting to reach out and grab you.

"Come on, Lovie."

"You go first. I'll be right behind you."

With my fierce watchdog trotting beside me still rumbling deep in his throat and Lovie dragging up the rear, we inch toward the front.

The setting sun shines through the vaulted window behind the pulpit, and the bank of stained glass windows in primary colors along the east wall glows softly as our feet move in carpeted hush. In spite of the peace and beauty of these surroundings, I don't want to find out what waits for us up front.

"Brian?"

I didn't really expect an answer. Taking a deep breath, I touch his shoulder and he topples off the bench, landing on his knees with his face flat against the floor.

"He's dead, Lovie."

"Either that or he's praying for the right notes."

Sometimes laughter is the only reason we can keep breathing. If I could bottle Lovie's spirit and sell it, I'd be rich.

Chapter 2

Motels, Mexico, and the Fatal Fox-Trot

I call Uncle Charlie on my cell phone; then Lovie and I debate who's going to tell the other impersonators Brian is dead and whether it's disrespectful to the leave the body unattended.

"You be the heroine if you want to, Callie, but I'm going outside till I can get my chocolate and my bladder under control."

"Uncle Charlie said he'd be right here. A few more minutes won't kill anybody." I hope. "I don't think we ought to leave him."

"What do you think he's going to do? Rise up and be raptured through the ceiling?"

She streamrolls toward the door with me racing along behind her. Outside, I stand a few minutes deep-breathing. I'm not cut out for this sort of thing. If God had wanted me to deal with the seamier side of life, He'd have put me in a family of hard-nosed cops and criminal lawyers instead of one that promotes beauty (me) and vodka (Lovie) and gives the job of official funeral home greeter to a dog.

Uncle Charlie arrives hard on the heels of the coroner.

"Wait out here, dear hearts. John will take care of things inside."

"What about the other impersonators?" Elvis is

now running around me in circles while Lovie sinks to the ground and fans herself with the tail of her skirt. "They're sitting in a hot bus wondering what happened."

"I'll handle things. When I get back, I'll take you two back into town."

As he sprints off toward the bus, I untangle my legs from the leash and sit down beside Lovie. "Are you okay?"

"I will be as soon as my stomach gets out of my throat."

"Brian can't be more than thirty. What do you suppose happened to him?"

"Whatever it is, Callie, it's none of our business."

"You're right." Visions of Lovie and me cramming a stiff into a freezer (a.k.a. the Bubbles Caper) are enough to make me keep my nose out of Brian Watson's demise.

Unless, of course, Uncle Charlie needs us. After all, he's in charge of this festival. (Well, practically.)

The coroner passes by with Brian's covered body strapped to a gurney. Uncle Charlie stops him a few yards away to chat.

I know it's none of my business, but I strain my ears anyway, hoping to hear what they're saying. "Natural causes," the coroner says, and "shipping the body back to Alabama."

Thank goodness nobody mentions foul play.

The coroner heads toward his van and Uncle Charlie joins us.

"Looks like it was a heart attack. Poor boy. I assured the other tribute artists the festival would not be canceled."

Which means the wine and cheese party I'm having tonight at my house in Mooreville will go on as planned. All the impersonators will be there as well as the fan club officers, the Elvis Committee members, Tupelo's mayor, Robert Earl Getty, and his wife, Junie Mae, the city council, and the bigwigs.

Not that I'm in a party mood, but it could be just the thing to take Lovie's mind off Brian's death. She's the best caterer in Mississippi. Any time there's a Valentine family function, she does the food. And nothing makes her feel better than being up to her elbows in grits soufflé and shrimp jambalaya.

Unless it's sex, and I refuse to go there. About her love life or my unfortunate attraction to my almost-ex, either one.

Uncle Charlie drives us back to get our vehicles. My Dodge Ram four-by-four with the Hemi engine (my *don't mess with me* alter ego) is parked near the historic courthouse square in the heart of downtown Tupelo.

I love this square. Daddy used to bring me here on Saturdays while Mama shopped downtown. We'd circle the hundred-year-old courthouse admiring the Civil War monument and the mysterious statue of the angel that nobody seems to know who put there. Then he'd boost me into the big magnolia tree on the northwest side of the square and stand underneath while I peered down at him through the waxy green leaves.

"I used to climb this tree, Callie. Someday your children will climb it."

As I get into my truck and head home I put my hands flat over my stomach to assure myself my eggs are still there. Humming their little cradle song. Just waiting for the right daddy to come along.

In case you're wondering, my white clapboard cottage in Mooreville is my dream house. It has a wraparound front porch with a beaded wood ceiling and old brick floors, porch rockers and wind chimes everywhere, a swing on the west end near the arbor spilling with Zephrine Drouhin (a French bourbon rose).

If you mentioned my house, you'd have to say it in the same breath as *southern charm*. That's the main reason most of the Valentine family socials, as well as more than a few civic events, are held here.

The first thing I do when I get home is turn on the stereo, which is already loaded with my favorite CDs—Eric Clapton's blues, Willie Nelson's whiskey-voiced ballads, and Marina

Raye's haunting Native American flute. Nothing fills up space and makes a house more welcoming than music.

Elvis ambles through the doggie door and into the backyard to lord it over my collection of stray animals—seven cats and Hoyt, the little blond spaniel. I haven't decided what to do about the cats, but I've decided to keep Hoyt. Hence, the name. Hoyt was one of Elvis' backup singers. Which ought to make my opinionated basset hound happy, but seems to have done just the opposite. From the kitchen window I spy Elvis sneaking off to his favorite oak tree to bury Hoyt's bone.

I push open the back screen door. "Elvis, give that back right this minute. You know you have plenty without stealing."

He gives me this *look,* then drops Hoyt's bone, huffs over to the gazebo, and plops down with his back to me. I swear, if I didn't know better I'd say he's been taking lessons from Mama. She wrote the book on *looks that can kill.*

"You know you're kidding. Be a good boy and don't torture Hoyt and the cats."

I race upstairs to change and shower. I can't wait to get out of these clothes. I'm sweaty from being in a tent on the hot asphalt of downtown Tupelo; plus, I feel tainted with death. *Poor Brian.*

Slipping into the shower, I close my eyes and

31

imagine the water washing my troubles down the drain. As I reach for the soap it's plucked from my hand.

"Here. Let me do that."

No use screaming. I know who it is before I turn around.

"Jack, need I remind you that you don't live here anymore? Need I also remind you that breaking and entering is a crime?"

His big laugh echoes off the tiled walls. "Who's going to scrub your back?" He starts slathering soap on me, and I swear if I could chop off his talented hands and keep only that part of him, I'd die a happy woman.

Well, maybe his talented tongue, too, but I'm not even going to think about that. If I do I'll end up in the middle of my own bed in a compromising position.

"Leave, Jack. And for goodness' sake, put on some clothes."

"Not before I say good-bye."

Suddenly his hands are everywhere and I end up on my bed, anyway. For a very long time.

What can I say? I'm not sorry. Jack may have terrible daddy potential, but he certainly excels at the preliminaries. And after all, I'm still married to him. Sort of.

Leaving me sprawled across the rumpled covers, he reaches for his pants. And I watch. I'll admit it. If there was anybody worth watching, it's Jack

Jones—six feet of muscle and mouth-watering appeal, and every inch of him lethal.

"I'm leaving town, Callie. I'll be gone awhile."

"For good, I hope."

"Is that why you're staring?" He plants a kiss that sizzles my roots, then strolls out the door like a swashbuckling Rhett Butler who just had his way with willful Scarlett.

And I'm back at square one—in the shower scrubbing off sweat.

"I thought you'd be dressed by now."

The soap slips out of my hand and I whirl around to face this new intrusion.

"Good grief, Mama. Don't you ever knock?"

"The front door was wide open."

She tosses me a towel, then makes herself at home while I towel off. I don't know another single person who could make the toilet seat look like a throne.

"I saw Jack." She gives me this *look*. If anybody can make you squirm, it's Mama. She has elevated stark raving silence to an art. "I told him to stay for the party. He's still part of the family."

"I never heard of family who went off whenever they pleased and didn't bother to tell you where they were going or what they were doing." Which is one of the many reasons I separated from Jack Jones. He could be a deep-cover assassin for all I know. "You shouldn't have invited him, Mama. It's my house."

"Really, Callie. Everbody knows you're still in love with him. Why can't you see that?"

I open the bathroom door. "Mama, do you mind? I have to pee."

"Don't let me stop you." Ignoring the door, she stations herself in front of my bathroom mirror and inspects her hair. "I'm thinking of going blond."

"For goodness' sake, Mama, you just went burnished copper."

"I'm thinking a Marilyn Monroe–ish look would go well with my dance costumes."

"What dance costumes?"

"Didn't I tell you?" *Naturally not.* Mama has secrets that would make you gray overnight. I guess that's why she's so crazy about Jack. They're two of a kind. "Fayrene and I have enrolled in a senior citizens' dance class. Everybody ought to expand their horizons, including you, my dear."

The only horizon I want to expand is to get a manicurist for Hair.Net, but that's hard to do. Every time I get a bit ahead, somebody comes along with a sob story. Mostly Mama, who usually needs *a little breather in Tunica* (her words, not mine). But I'll have to say that subsidizing her occasional gambling jaunts is a small price to pay for having a mother who is larger than life.

Life with Mama is never boring. And if either one of us ended up in front of a speeding train, the

34

other would step in and take her place on the tracks.

She follows me into the bedroom trailing Hawaiian ginger perfume and hot-pink ruffles while I slip into a yellow sundress and matching Michael Kors ballerina flats. Designer shoes always perk me up, and after today's events at the chapel, I need all the help I can get.

We head down the stairs just as Lovie breezes in with the party food and her overnight bag. (She's spending the night with me, which is not unusual. If she's staying late in Mooreville or I'm staying late in Tupelo, we crash at each other's houses.)

Fayrene is right behind her. When I lift my eyebrows, Lovie winks at me.

"Fayrene said she came early to help."

Snoop is more like it. Fayrene loves to be in the know. But I'm more than happy to leave arranging the food to Mama and her coconspirator in dance and devilment because Lovie is motioning me behind their backs.

We slip out of the kitchen and into my living room. Actually it's two rooms with vaulted ceilings and the adjoining wall knocked out, dominated by my antique baby grand piano. When you enter you have the feeling of being in Thomas Jefferson's elegant Monticello.

"What gives, Lovie?"

"Rocky called again. He's booked a room at the Ramada."

"It's a nice hotel."

"Why doesn't he want to stay with me, Callie? He'll just be here a few days and then he's flying to Mexico on a dig." Rocky's an archaeologist who apparently has more passion for treasures of the past than the treasure right before his eyes. "He'll be gone no telling how long. What am I going to do?"

Asking me for love advice is like asking a sinner to preach at a Baptist church revival. I wrote the book on *how not to*. Still, I can't be flippant with Lovie. For the first time since Aunt Minrose died (Lovie was fourteen), she is thinking of men in terms of commitment instead of a Band-Aid to tape over the wound of loss.

"It looks like Rocky wants to move slowly, Lovie. And that might be a good idea."

"I'm not interested in *slow*. I want a little sugar in my bowl."

How like Lovie to use the language of the blues. Aunt Minrose was a professional musician and Lovie's no slouch, herself.

"Focus on the bright side. I'll bet he's bringing not only the sugar but a big stirring spoon."

Mama sticks her head around the door frame. "To stir what?"

"The Prohibition Punch," Lovie says, referring to her special recipe that parades itself as punch but has enough alcohol to make a herd of elephants tipsy. Actually the recipe originated with a gov-

36

ernor's wife in Georgia during the Prohibition Era.

Lovie squeezes my arm, then swishes past me to the kitchen while I race to answer the front door.

Standing on my porch are Tupelo's mayor and his wife, and behind them are Beulah Jane and twenty bespangled, pomaded impersonators.

By seven thirty the party is in full swing. The bigwigs are crowded around the refreshment table refilling their cups with Lovie's recipe and loosening their ties. Fayrene is in my Angel Garden/ courtyard matching Beulah Jane and the officers of the fan club with Elvis stories of her own. (Fayrene claims to be Gladys' niece's second cousin twice removed). And Mama's at the piano pounding out Elvis songs while the impersonators try to outdo each other showing off their vocals and their hip moves. George Blakely, a skinny balloonist from Dallas who calls himself Texas Elvis, seems to have the corner on swivels.

The real King strolls in (my dog, who else?) carrying a black wig he dug from my closet when I wasn't looking. Elvis is the most opinionated dog on earth. Obviously, he has a point to prove. I bend down, take it from his teeth, and arrange it on his head, then lavish pats on him.

"You look mighty handsome, Elvis." My philosophy is that everybody needs affirmation, even a dog.

"Here, dear heart. You look like you need this."

Uncle Charlie hands me a fresh cup of Prohibition Punch.

"It's not every day I see a dead Elvis in the Birthplace. Have you heard anything else about Brian?"

"John's sticking by his on-site evaluation of natural causes. The body has already been released to his family in Huntsville."

That ought to make me feel better, but I still have the uneasy feeling I'm on the *Titanic* while an iceberg lurks just beyond the next wave. I don't know. Maybe it's the turmoil of my love/hate relationship with Jack and our stalled divorce.

"Don't worry about it, dear heart. Everything's under control. Enjoy your party."

In spite of his reassurances, Uncle Charlie stations himself in my blue velvet wing chair in the corner. He's either found a perfect observation post because something is amiss, or he's watching for trouble just to be on the safe side.

Going in search of comfort, I find Lovie in the kitchen refilling a serving tray with hot miniature ham and cheese quiches. I grab a spatula to help, but end up dropping quiche on the floor.

"Let me do that." Lovie elbows me out of the way. "Are you going to tell me what's up, or are you going to spend the rest of the evening with that face?"

"It's the only face I have."

"You know what I mean. What's up?"

"Nothing if you don't count Mama taking clandestine dance lessons and me letting Jack back in my bed."

"Don't worry about it, Callie. Divorced people do it all the time."

"How do you know?"

"Trust me. I know these things. Besides, at least Jack finds you appealing."

"Lovie, Rocky has been crazy about you ever since he saw you imitating a Las Vegas showgirl."

"How do you know?"

"You told me. Besides, you've been seeing him . . . what? Two weeks?"

"Three. They build Jim Walter homes in less time. At the rate he's going, I'll be in dentures and Depends before he discovers the holy grail."

This is Lovie at her irreverent best. Anybody who didn't know her might think she's taking everything in stride, but I see the heartache behind the laughter.

Elvis (the icon, not my dog) is crooning "It's Now or Never" over my indoor/outdoor speakers, which is the last thing Lovie needs to hear. Apparently Mama has abandoned the piano and put on some Elvis CDs.

"What you need is some fresh air."

Lovie's a party animal. If I can get her surrounded by people, she'll be okay. Linking arms, we head to the courtyard I call my Angel Garden.

This place always makes me feel better.

Sometimes in the early morning if I come out here and sit very still, I can feel the brush of angel wings. Not that I'm New Age-y or anything. I just believe you have to adopt a Zen-like state of stillness in order to be in touch with the universe.

Tonight, though, angel wings take a powder because there's Mama in dishabille, so to speak, with Texas Elvis. Actually, they're dancing—if you can call being crammed so close you can't get a straw between your bodies *dancing*. Plus, his hands are where they have no business being.

The worst part is, she doesn't seem to mind, which leads me to believe this could have been her idea. If she'll care to remember, she has a daughter older than this man. To top it off, this is my house, and I'm not fixing to let this gold-digging Elvis swivel his way into a beautiful farm in Mooreville. Not to mention Mama's Everlasting Monument Company and a place at the Valentine family Thanksgiving dinner.

Besides that, he's not even handsome. How could Mama go for a weasely man who looks like Pee-Wee Herman?

I march right into my house and remove the *Burning Love* album. I don't care how many times it went platinum. I have no intention of providing the ambience for Lady Chatterly. Next I put on "Shake, Rattle and Roll." Let Mama and George Blakley cozy up to that.

"What's wrong, dear heart?"

I jump out of my skin. How did Uncle Charlie get across the room without me ever seeing him move?

"Nobody but Mama could turn dance lessons into something you have to worry over."

He doesn't say a word, just slips out the door with his blue eyes looking like they could burn a hole through metal. Now what?

I hurry after Uncle Charlie and find him leading Mama back onto the dance floor while George Blakely cools his ardor on the sidelines with a glass of peach tea.

The courtyard has been cleared to make way for a second dance couple. None other than Lovie with Dick Gerard.

Who is married, might I add. And whose wife, Bertha, is not here.

I can see my party being written up in the society pages as the biggest scandal Moorevile has seen since Leonora Moffett stole Roy Jessup's daddy from the Mooreville Feed and Seed. Even worse, she didn't want him. Sent him back to his wife in three weeks because he *had the IQ of a snail.* Leonora's words, not mine.

All I can say is *thank goodness* the hip-hop music prevents Lovie from dancing cheek to cheek with Dick. Though the way she's rocking (all over the courtyard) and the way he's rolling (all over her), my party ought to be rated triple X.

What in the world is Lovie trying to do? As if I need to ask. Feeling uncertain about Rocky's intentions and floundering around in unfamiliar territory, she's falling back into her old habits— seeing how many men she can conquer with her charms (which are considerable, believe me).

But who am I to talk? Don't I let Jack sweet-talk me every time? What can I say? There's comfort in the familiar.

In order to preserve my sanity (almost) and calm my nerves (barely), I watch Uncle Charlie and Mama. She's a really good dancer, which doesn't surprise me. Whatever Mama sets her mind to, she does with gusto and excellence. The surprise here is Uncle Charlie. I had no idea he could dance, much less that he's so smooth. With that talent and his handsome, silvery fox looks, he could have senior women drooling all over him.

Suddenly somebody yells, "What's happening?"

Lovie and Dick are gyrating so wildly that Mama and Uncle Charlie quit the dance floor. If I couldn't see the panic on Lovie's face, I'd think she was doing this on purpose.

"Uncle Charlie," I yell, but he has already sprung into action. When Dick Gerard topples, he lands right in Charlie Valentine's arms.

While Tewanda Hardy and Beulah Jane fan Dick with their cardboard Elvis fans, I race inside to get some ice water and a cold cloth.

Considering the heat, no wonder he's overcome. Not to mention the potency of Lovie's charms and her Prohibition Punch.

By the time I get back, my bassett hound is on the scene and Dick is laid out on the concrete.

Uncle Charlie looks up from the body. "It's no use, dear heart. He's dead."

Elvis' Opinion #2 on Icons, Hospitality, and Murder

I could have told them that before Dick Gerard hit the floor. But then, I'm smarter than the average dog. What I saw was not a man in the throes of dance; it was a man in the throes of a fit.

With sirens wailing toward Callie's, everybody's standing around the body saying, "I told you so."

Tewanda Hardy is saying, "I told you it was an epileptic fit," while Fayrene is saying, "It looked more like he got stung by a bee."

Even that uppity cocker spaniel is nosing around trying to act important. Need I remind him that Callie named him Hoyt because of *me*? I'm the only icon around here, and if he wants some peace in the valley, he'll do well to remember it.

Before he got his own pillow and tried to horn in my territory, I was starting to warm up to him. Even considered teaching a thing or two about music, but that's gone with the wind now. I may be the most beloved dog in Mooreville, not to mention the coolest, but I have my limits.

Hoyt will have to fend for himself. Ditto, this untalented, ragtag group of impersonators. There was a moment this morning after competition got under way that I considered moseying around their tent and offering remedial voice lessons. But after hearing Brian Watson I figured, *why waste my valuable time?* It would take an act of God to improve the singing of this sorry lot.

Now, if you listen to this party crowd jabbering, you're probably thinking God has already intervened, but let me tell you . . . Brian and Dick did not die of natural causes. Ask the best canine detective in the world (that would be yours truly); two dead impersonators add up to murder.

To prove my point, Callie's front yard is filled with flashing blue lights. There're more cops here than I have fleas. And they're everywhere.

While the Lee County sheriff and two of his deputies clear Callie's courtyard and put crime scene tape around it and the coroner hauls Dick off, Hoyt starts howling "Love Me Tender."

I politely priss my ample butt over there and tell him to knock it off. Any fool knows it's tasteless to sing the wrong song. Besides, he can't even sing backup. What makes him think he can sing solo?

And speaking of singing, the two deceased impersonators were the worst of the lot. If you ask me (which, of course, nobody does), anybody who makes my songs sound that bad ought to be grateful they're dead.

Chapter 3

Clues, Mistaken Identity, and the Dead Dick

*C*rime scene tape in my own backyard. I wonder if that would hold up in a divorce court as proof I'm an unfit dog mother. All I can say is that I'm glad Jack's out of town.

Even worse, my guests are milling around, shell-shocked, and the assorted Elvises are in a near riot. The one from Georgia is threatening to go home, the one from California is threatening to sue somebody, and the one from Japan is behind my gardenia bush pulling a stiletto out of his boots.

While the sheriff and his deputies ask questions and take notes, the Valentines gather in the kitchen for a summit. Lovie's already dumping vodka in the Prohibition Punch and Mama adds enough sherry to float a small boat.

"Good," Uncle Charlie says. "Pass it around."

"Maybe I ought to turn off the music." My house and gardens sound like the inside of a boot and skoot club.

"Leave it on, dear heart. The more normal we can seem, the better."

"What are you going to do about the festival, Charlie?"

In spite of the bad advice Mama gives me and

the bad judgment she uses in her own affairs, when caution and wisdom really count, she defers to Uncle Charlie.

"I'm going to announce that unfortunate events in Mooreville don't mean cancelation of the festival in Tupelo."

As he leaves, Mama follows him to the door. "Be careful, Charlie. There's a murderer on the loose."

She comes back and I press close to her and Lovie while we fill cups with the spiked punch. When George Blakely sticks his head around the door and booms out, "Hello," I send punch flying onto the ceiling. Then I stand there under the drip like somebody nailed to the floor.

"Sorry." He grabs a napkin and starts wiping punch out of my hair. "I just wanted to see if everybody is all right."

Lovie gives me a look and I know exactly what she means. *Snooping. We'd better keep an eye on this one.* You don't grow up sharing the same sandbox and the same quilt at sleepovers without learning to read the other person's mind.

"I'm fine." I step out of George's reach. His hands give me the creeps. Probably because he had them all over Mama. "What can I do for you?"

"The sheriff was asking about Lovie. I think he wants to question her."

Mama links her arm through his. "George, you be a good boy and march right out there and tell

47

Sheriff Trice, Lovie will be there when she's good and ready."

"I don't know, Ruby girl."

Girl? I could slap him.

"Well, I do. There are plenty of people at this party to question first without him trying to put my niece on the hot seat. If he knows what's good for his next election campaign, he'll treat the Valentines with a little respect. And you can tell him I said so."

"Yes, ma'am!" Grinning, George salutes Mama, then hurries off to do her bidding.

"Mama, what's up with you and that impersonator?"

"Oh, was something up? I didn't notice."

She prisses off with a tray, all flouncy ruffles and big attitude. I wouldn't dye her hair Marilyn Monroe blond if you took away my Jimmy Choo sling-backs. Mama gets in enough trouble as a red-head.

"I might as well get our there and face the music." Lovie grabs a tray and starts out the door.

"Not without me, you don't."

The sheriff is taking notes while Fayrene holds court on my porch swing. The porch is crowded with people trying to eavesdrop but look like they're not, and the scent of Zephrine Drouhin roses from the nearby arbor is heavy on the still summer air.

"Of course Lovie was dancing with Dick Gerard, but she didn't do anything to him." Fayrene glares at Sheriff Trice like she'd love to skewer him and serve him as shish kabobs. "Ask anybody here. The Valentine family is above reproach."

"Ma'am, just stick to the facts. What did you see?"

"I saw Dick's jealous wife, Bertha, hiding behind the Confederate jasmine watching them dance in the courtyard. That's what I saw."

"Are you sure it was Bertha Gerard?"

"I never forget a face. I have a pornographic memory."

Several of the impersonators snicker, but the sheriff remains straight-faced. A local who gets his gas as well as his fish bait at Gas, Grits, and Guts, he knows Fayrene is the queen of malapropisms.

"When was the last time you saw Bertha?"

"I just told you," Fayrene says.

"Before tonight."

"It was three weeks ago. At the dentist's. I was just getting ready to go under Anastasia."

The mayor and his wife are choking on their Prohibition Punch, and Italian Elvis is frantically consulting his pocket translation guide.

The sheriff turns to me. "Was Bertha on the guest list?"

"Yes," I say, "but she called early this morning to say she couldn't come."

"Did she say why?"

"She said she was sick."

"Did she sound sick?"

Good grief, what am I now? A doctor?

"She wasn't coughing and I didn't detect any nasal stuffiness, but she could have had an upset stomach. I really can't say."

The sheriff walks off to consult Deputy Rakestraw while Fayrene sits there looking miffed. Probably because the sheriff didn't take her word as gospel. Mama goes over to lend Fayrene moral support.

Meanwhile Sheriff Trice comes up to me and asks for a private room to question Lovie. What would he do if I told him I didn't allow the enemy into my private quarters? Put me in jail, probably.

I lead them into my kitchen, which is Lovie's natural habitat. If she's going to be the prime suspect just because she was dancing with the deceased, the least I can do is give her an edge during the interrogation.

"Can I sit in for the interrogation?" It's my house. I don't see why not.

"I'm sorry. This one has to be in private."

Before I close the kitchen door I see Lovie reaching for a chocolate éclair. She's going to be all right.

That's what I'm telling myself when Mama and Fayrene walk in and catch me still standing at the kitchen door.

"Are you eavesdropping?" When I tell Mama *no,* she says, "Why not?"

She and Fayrene grab two of my crystal glasses off the coffee table, dump the leftover wine into my potted peace lily, then proceed to put the rim to the kitchen wall.

I grab a glass and follow suit. But not before I lock the front door so we won't get caught. Listen, if this was the worst thing I'd ever done, I'd be nominated for sainthood. And we all know that's not going to happen.

"Did you notice anything strange when you were dancing with Dick?" I hear the sheriff asking Lovie.

"No. Not at first. The music was loud, rock 'n' roll, and I was really into it."

"You said *not at first.*"

"Yes. I thought something was amiss when he began to lean heavily on me. Then I realized he wasn't gyrating to the beat."

"What was Dick doing?"

"I'm no doctor, but I'd say he had a seizure of some kind."

"You're in charge of the food here. Is that correct?"

"Yes. I always cater the Valentine parties."

"What about the festival? Are you in charge of the refreshment booth?"

"Not really. The officers of the Elvis fan club are in charge of it."

51

"That would be . . ."

"Beulah Jane Ball, Tewanda Hardy, Clytee Estes, and James Holman."

"Who provided the food for the booth?"

Holy cow! It's Lovie, of course. Any southerner worth his salt who wants the best always uses Lovie's Luscious Eats.

The sheriff is building a case for murder right in my kitchen. And all I can do is stand outside the door and wait.

Mama, of course, has other ideas. "I'm going to march in there and snatch him bald-headed."

She grabs the door handle and I pull her back in the nick of time. Putting my finger to my lips, I lean in to pick up the thread of interrogation.

"Did you know Dick before this festival?"

"Yes," Lovie says. "He delivers my mail."

"Is that all he delivers?"

There's a long pause, which means something's up. Probably something I'm not going to like.

"We were lovers."

Lovie tells me everything. Why didn't I know about Dick?

"But that was a long time ago, before he married Bertha," she's saying. "Until this festival, I hadn't seen nor spoken privately to Dick in six months."

"So he jilted you?"

"No. He did not."

"The two of you broke up and you had hard feelings."

"The only beef I have against Dick Gerard is that he scatters my mail all the way from Church Street to Highland Circle."

Chairs scrape against my kitchen floor, and we jump into action. I put the telltale glasses on a tray on the coffee table, then race to unlock the front door while Fayrene grabs a book off the shelves and pretends to be reading. Mama plops onto the piano bench and starts belting out "Suspicious Minds."

Leave it to Mama. Sheriff Trice, who knows his Elvis, glares at her, but she just winks and keeps on warbling. Normally her voice is pure as rain, but considering the kind of pressure we've suffered this evening, she's considerably off-key.

The sheriff comes over to me and says, "Callie, can you point out that Confederate jasmine bush?"

I lead him back to the courtyard and point out the bush. While the deputies search for clues and gather food and drink samples, Uncle Charlie pulls Sheriff Trice aside to request that the guests be allowed to leave.

Very few people can get by with telling the law how to do their job, but everybody has deep respect for Uncle Charlie, including Sheriff Trice.

"B. B. King is in concert tonight at the Elvis Festival," Uncle Charlie tells him. "It's a pity for all these people to miss it if they don't have to. Especially our international guests."

"They're free to go."

"And my daughter?"

While his deputies are loading up the food samples and little plastic bags of whatever evidence they've found, the sheriff puts his hand on Uncle Charlie's arm. "Mr. Valentine, with two impersonators dead on the same day and both of them in their prime, we'll treat this as a criminal case until the autopsy shows otherwise. Right now we don't have enough evidence for an arrest, but I'd appreciate it if you'll see that your daughter doesn't leave Lee County."

With those chilling words, Sheriff Trice and his deputies get into their patrol cars and leave. In short order my house and grounds are clear of everybody except family.

Gathered on the front porch watching the last of the blue lights flash down the street, we don't say anything.

Lovie is suspected of murder. It's like having a big pink elephant in the porch swing. We all know it's there, but nobody wants to be the one to acknowledge it.

Finally Uncle Charlie stands up, puts his hands in his pockets, and rattles his car keys, a habit when he's trying to sort things out. " 'Better to leave undone than by our deed acquire too high a fame.' "

He's quite a scholar and always quotes Shakespeare, especially in time of stress. That's his way of telling us to be still and let the law catch the killer.

"Ruby Nell, are you ready to go?" Uncle Charlie's talking about the blues concert, which is this evening's main event at the Elvis Festival.

"I'm always ready, Charlie."

If I needed any proof that Mama meant her double entendre, all I have to do is look at her wicked grin.

In his courtly way, Uncle Charlie offers Mama his arm. "Relax, dear hearts. We're going to hold our heads high and get through the rest of the festival in true Valentine fashion."

After Uncle Charlie and Mama leave, Lovie and I make a beeline for the Prohibition Punch. I guess you could say that when *true Valentine fashion* was passed around, I was at a fifty-percent-off sale looking for Juicy Couture shoes and Lovie was in the bedroom searching for the right man to appreciate her holy grail.

Elvis strolls through the doggie door with Hoyt trailing along behind. I remove my basset's wig and bow tie, then give them both a doggie treat.

Lovie says a word that sends Hoyt scurrying under the table.

"What?" I put the box of Milk-Bone back on the shelf, then refill our glasses.

"You know what this means, Callie?"

"We'll have hangovers?"

"We've got to find the real killer."

She's right, of course. With one successful (more or less) bit of detective work behind us, we're primed to sleuth. And I know just where to start.

Chapter 4

Rhinestones, Half-Baked Plans, and Moaning Strangers

Grabbing flashlights (which I have two of, thanks to Jack Jones, who believes in always being prepared), I drag Lovie back to the courtyard.

"We're not supposed to cross the crime scene tape," she says.

"How are we going to find clues if we don't?"

"The deputies already searched there."

"Everybody in Lee County knows Fayrene doesn't know a Confederate jasmine from a warthog. Besides, everybody's already tromped all over my courtyard. What will two more hurt?"

"You know what I always say."

Lovie and I give each other the high five while we chant, *"If nobody sees you, you didn't do it."* Then we clamber over the yellow tape.

On our hands and knees, we train flashlights onto every inch of ground *except* that around the Confederate jasmine. In spite of the sophistication I have single-handedly brought to Mooreville— candles banked on the tables (which the sheriff's deputies already snuffed out) and white lights strung around every bush and tree—there's not enough illumination to find clues on the ground in the dark without added light.

I adore being in my gardens, especially at night. I've made sure the artificial lights don't overpower nature. Nothing is more soothing than lying in my Pauley's Island hammock watching the stars and moon, reveling in the beauty and power of the universe. Everything is in perspective then, life's tribulations reduced to a speck of dust.

Except murder, of course. And maybe those involving Jack. Whom I would give my eyeteeth to see right now.

In spite of his flaws—which are legion—he had a way of making me feel safe. And still does when I'm not too mad at him to notice. I don't know. Sometimes the only reason you can breathe is that somebody holds you close and says *everything is going to be all right.*

Which brings me back to the current dilemma. If I thought losing Lovie to a split-level in Las Vegas and three children would be tough, what about losing her to Parchman Penitentiary and prison chef?

Behind me there's a crash. Training my flashing light in that direction, I see Lovie sprawled on the ground under my tea olive.

I race over to pull her up. No easy task. "Are you all right?"

"I will be if I can get out of this ant bed."

While I brush dirt and twigs off the seat of her skirt, she says a word that's good practice for being a hardened criminal.

"Did they bite you?"

"Are you kidding? After being crushed by this ass the little suckers are down there burying their dead." She plops into a chair. "I'm not built for squatting. You'll have to look for clues by yourself."

So far I've turned up nothing except a half-buried chew toy. Elvis's work, I'm sure. He's so determined not to share with Hoyt, he deprives himself of the pleasure of his doggie toys by trying to put them six feet under.

I'm beginning to think this search is hopeless, that Fayrene made up the Bertha-behind-the-bush story to get in the limelight. But I don't say this to Lovie. She needs to think we're making progress in clearing her name.

Elvis, who reads minds and knows when somebody's hurting, prances over to Lovie and licks her foot, then joins me and starts nosing under the tea olive. Dropping to one knee, I shine my flashlight in his direction.

"I found something." Scooping it up, I sit beside Lovie and hold out my palm. Resting inside is a rhinestone hairpin.

She leans forward to inspect it. "Do you think it belongs to Bertha?"

"It could be. There's only one way to find out."

"Find out where she lives, then break and enter."

Lovie and I slap palms. Lucky for us, Lovie dated "Slick Fingers" Johnson, who was always one step ahead of the law. One of the many things she learned from him was how to pick locks.

I change into a black outfit cat burglars would wear while Lovie changes into the jeans and navy T-shirt she brought; then we search the telephone book looking for Dick Gerard's address. There are two Richards and two Dicks. The only problem is we don't know which one is the dead Dick.

"We'll just have to call and find out." I glance at the clock. It's not quite ten, still early enough to call without being impolite.

"If we use your phone or either of our cell phones, anybody with caller ID can finger us."

There Lovie goes again, speaking in film noir. When we accidentally got into detective work via the Bubbles Caper, she started sounding like Dick Powell in *Farewell, My Lovely* and Humphrey Bogart in *Dark Passage.* Of course, this is not surprising since one of our favorite pastimes is kicking back with a big bowl of buttered popcorn, watching the classic movies on TV. Hers or mine. It doesn't matter as long as we watch together.

Now here we are, up to our necks in murder again, formulating a plan as we race to Gas, Grits, and Guts to use the pay phone outside.

The plan is for me to make the calls because Lovie's Luscious Eats is all but famous and so is her sexy drawl. Think Kathleen Turner with a Marlene Dietrich twist. The cover story is that I'm doing a feasibility study for Ole Miss regarding a continuing education course on global warming at the Tupelo campus. Lovie wanted to make it a Masters and Johnsons type of survey, but common sense (mine) prevailed.

As I wheel my monster truck into the parking lot, I notice Fayrene's husband, Jarvetis, through the plate-glass windows. Thank goodness he's the one closing the store tonight instead of his wife, who would barrel out bent on sniffing out our mission. Even worse, she'd want to *help*. Like Mama, Fayrene doesn't know the meaning of *discreet*.

I park as far away from the door as I can get. As I get out of the truck, I hear the distant rumble of thunder. My gardens need rain, the farmers need rain, everybody needs rain except two amateur detectives who have enough trouble without skulking around in a downpour.

"You can wait in the truck if you want to, Lovie."

She clambers out behind me. "I'm the one knocking off old lovers."

"Good grief. Brian was your lover, too?"

"No, but if I'd met him before he kicked the bucket, he would have been."

I think she's kidding, but sometimes it's hard to tell. Lovie has had her share of *experiences,* but she also covers up a lot of deep feelings with jokes and laughter.

We pool our quarters and I start making calls. I get voice mails with the two Richards and a propo-

61

sition with the first Dick. He lives on Enoch, never heard of Bertha, and thinks I'm his twenty-first birthday present from his buddies at the factory.

On the final try we find the dead Dick's unfortunate wife. In 225 Magnolia Manor. Jack's apartment building.

I stand in by the pay phone thinking about that tacky yellow brick building with the pretentious name and the socially unacceptable address. Cracked asphalt parking lot. One pitiful pine. Not a flower in sight. As far as I know, not even a blade of grass.

And Jack, who loves gardens and cool breezes and porch swings, is living there. All because of me. Well, because of him, too. But still . . .

"I can't go barging into Magnolia Manor, Lovie. What if I run into Jack?"

"I thought you said he was leaving town."

"For all I know he caught a magic carpet and has already made a trip to Tibet and back. Besides, he didn't say *when* he was leaving. My point is, I don't want him to know what we're up to."

"We're going to be up to our asses in rain, if we don't hurry."

A crack of thunder underscores her prediction as we race to the truck. I peel out of the parking lot just in time to be spotted by Jarvetis. That means he'll tell Fayrene, who will tell Mama, who might tell Jack. Not that Mama would betray me, but she'll do anything she can to get us back together. Because of my daddy, Michael Valentine, she believes in one true soul mate, and in her opinion, Jack is mine.

If I thought that, I'd just give up and my poor unused eggs would go out and commit suicide.

Rain sprinkles my windshield as I drive west toward Magnolia Manor.

"I don't know why I'm doing this," I say. "We can't just go barging down the hall for you to pick the lock."

"We should have worn disguises."

"I could be wearing an elephant suit and Jack would recognize me."

"Maybe I can do this by myself."

"Yeah? And how will you explain yourself when Jack catches you breaking and entering?"

Lovie says a word I'll bet even the devil doesn't know. "You're getting paranoid, Callie. Jack's out of town. And if he's not, we'll lie."

"Oh, right. Like he won't know."

She says another word, even worse. "Fetuses can hear," I tell her.

"Are you telling me you're pregnant?"

"No, but someday I will be. You don't want to pollute the ears of your little goddaughter."

"Give me two weeks' notice and I'll quit. Are you satisfied now?"

"Maybe." Actually I won't be satisfied till I'm home in my bed. I don't like the idea of being in Jack's territory in the dark. "I can tell you one thing. I'm not sleeping with him again."

"I didn't know you *slept*."

"That's mean, Lovie. And you know that's not what I meant."

"Okay. Forget I said that."

The entrance to Magnolia Manor looms ahead. I press down on the accelerator.

"You passed it, Callie."

"I know. I'm thinking."

"Of what?"

"A way to get to the second floor without being seen." And I think I just might have it. If the tree is in the right place.

I turn around in the parking lot of the Putt-Putt golf course next door, then head back to the Magnolia Manor. It's even uglier than I remembered, the yellow brick getting dingy, the hideous brown shutters peeling, and the dinky wrought-iron balconies looking like they're about to fall off the side of the building.

A postage-stamp patch of dirt surrounds the building, which sits in the middle of the parking lot. The lonesome pine presses close to the yellow brick. Right where I remembered.

"You see that tree?" I ask Lovie. "It's near Jack's window. He's in 221, which means Bertha is two doors down."

I bail out of the truck, but she sits there like she's hatching eggs. I stick my head back in the cab. "What?"

"The only elephant I ever saw in a tree was

Dumbo. The next thing I know, you'll be telling me I can fly."

"We grew up climbing trees, Lovie."

"Yeah, but I was thirty years younger and a hundred pounds lighter."

"Well, all right, then. You sit here. I'll do it myself."

I've gone only half a dozen yards when Lovie catches up. I knew she would. We've been a team since Lovie beat the tar out of Johnny Lipscomb in the sandbox in Ballard Park for stealing my pail. She was four, I was three.

"I'm going to sue somebody if I fall," she says.

"You're not going to fall. I'll go first."

I know I sound brave, but believe me, if healthy thirty-seven-year-olds could have heart attacks from fright, I'd already be dead. To say this tree is spindly is putting it mildly. These branches look like they wouldn't hold a squirrel, let alone a hairstylist with a harebrained scheme and a hundred-and-ninety-pound bombshell. In addition, they're slick with rain.

Not to mention that Jack has probably already picked up my scent and is getting ready to do no telling what.

"Let's just go home, Callie, and forget it."

I almost take her advice. But I'm no quitter. "Shh. We have to be quiet." In the dead of night in this heavy humidity, there's no telling how far our voices carry.

65

Reaching for a limb, I swing myself upward. My foot slips and I can see the headlines: *Death by Tree*.

Silently calling on every deity I know and a few I don't, I hang on. "Come on up," I whisper. "It's fine."

Lovie is more athletic than she looks. Though I'm taller and skinnier, she can outrun me by two lengths. And growing up on the farm, she could always outclimb me.

Tonight she proves she still has what it takes to conquer a tree. In spite of rain, fear, and excess baggage, we gain the uppermost branches, then sit there with the tree swaying.

"Which window?" she whispers.

From this perspective, I have no idea. But I'm not about to tell Lovie. She'd say a word that would wake everybody in Magnolia Manor.

"We're right under it." Of course, I could be wrong.

I swing my leg over the balcony rail and hear a tiny *clunk*.

"What was that?" Lovie whispers.

"My car keys." Hitting the ground.

She says a word that perfectly expresses my feelings. I wish it was in my vocabulary.

There's no time to climb back down and search for keys. Besides, who's going to find them? Lovie and I are the only ones breaking and entering in the middle in a rainstorm. Well, it's not actually a storm, but it's getting worse.

I haul myself over the railing, then reach out to help Lovie. The wrought iron creaks alarmingly.

"Quick, Lovie."

Before we fall, is what I'm thinking, but she's through the window before I can even finish the thought. I follow, then stand there letting my eyes adjust to the dark.

Suddenly somebody or *something* moans. Lovie and I grab each other and freeze.

"What's that?" she whispers.

"A cat?"

The scream we hear next is no cat. It's a woman. And judging by the sound, she's being murdered.

The only good thing I can say is that we're not in Jack's apartment.

Elvis' Opinion #3 on Cocker Spaniels, Sleeping Arrangements, and Rat Poison

You'd think after all the excitement around here, a dog could get a decent night's sleep. But *no*. I'm having to put up with that upstart cocker spaniel. Just because Callie bought him a personalized doggie bed, he thinks he owns the bedroom.

Don't think I didn't see him nosing it around the end of Callie's bed trying to get on my side. Next thing you know he'll be trying to claim credit for my recording career. That'll be all she wrote.

With my sophistication and savoir faire, I may look like I breezed to success on the back of somebody's rich coattails, but let me tell you, I'm a dog who learned the hard way. While I was a skinny teenager gyrating and singing "Keep Your Hands off of It" at the government housing project in Memphis, Tennessee (Lauderdale Courts to be exact), I was learning to back up my actions with my fists.

I may be a tad paunchy now (if I don't suck my stomach in), but I can still put Hoyt six feet under.

I get off my private pillow (guitar shaped and embroidered with my name *and* a TCB thunderbolt, thank you, thank you very much), prance my ample butt around the corner of the footboard, and growl like I mean business. Hoyt gives me this dumb cocker spaniel look, then tries to lick my face. He'd better learn he's dealing with a King who grew up the hard way.

And if fisticuffs fail, there's always Ruby Nell's rat poison.

Speaking of which, I wonder if that's what somebody used to knock off the two impersonators. After those sorry performances over in Tupelo, I'd have done it myself if I could have found an escape hole in the fence and Ruby Nell's stash.

If I didn't know her so well, I'd say she killed them. Callie's mama does not suffer fools, and anybody who puts on my signature jumpsuit and then slaughters my songs falls into that category.

Anyhow, the rhinestone hairpin I found is not Ruby Nell's style.

Okay, so I let Callie think *she* found it. Listen, anybody suffering a broken heart and a near-terminal case of worry needs all the affirmation she can get. Since Jack left it's a full-time job around here.

She puts on a good front and everybody thinks she's this naturally cheerful spirit, but I can smell blues a mile. I know what I know. A dog's sacred duty is to make sure his human mom feels well loved and understands her own worth.

I excel at these things.

Just as Ruby Nell excels at never growing old. And why should she? Unless, of course, she could be reincarnated as a basset hound.

Chapter 5

Sex, Valium, and the Big Bad Wolf

L et's get out of here." Lovie inches toward the window and I'm right behind her. Two murders in one day are enough.

"Bill, did you hear something?" It's a woman's voice coming from behind a closed door.

"What'd you say, Gertrude?"

"I said somebody's out there."

The door pops open and Lovie and I scuttle behind a damask drapery. But not before I get a good look at Bill and Gertrude. If they're dressed for murder, I'm Jack the Ripper.

In wire-rim glasses and nightcap (Gertrude) and a mask with wicked fangs and a rubber snout (Bill), they make an unforgettable Grandma and the Big Bad Wolf. *Unforgettable* because they're naked as boiled eggs—and judging by the evidence, at least eighty-five.

Geriatric sex just took on a whole new meaning.

Lovie's choking with suppressed laughter and I poke her in the ribs. All we need is to be discovered behind the draperies and pressed into service as Little Red Riding Hood.

"I don't see anybody, Gertrude."

"You didn't look, you old fool."

"I'm too busy looking at you. Come here,

Grandma." It sounds like he's chasing her around the room. "Tell me what big teeth I have."

There's a thump, then silence. They've either landed in a heap or keeled over dead from excitement.

"What's happening?" Lovie whispers.

I peer around the curtain and see Grandma and the Big Bad Wolf on the sofa doing things I'm too embarrassed to talk about. Ducking back, I stir up dust and a huge sneeze. That's all I need.

I pinch my nose to hold it back. Do sneezes implode and blow people's brains out?

"Ohhh," Gertrude is saying. "Big Bad Wolfie, what big teeth you have."

"The better to eat you with."

There's a little pause, then that scream again. Only this time I know it's not murder. Plus, it covers the sneeze I can no longer hold in.

"Now what?" Lovie whispers.

"We wait them out."

I think about shoes. Any kind of shoes so long as they're designer, so long as they take my mind off the sounds of Grandma and the Big Bad Wolf. I'm lusting over a pair of Franco Sarto suede ankle boots I saw at the hairdressers' convention in Atlanta last week when I hear the bedroom door close.

I guess it's the bedroom door. Where else would they be going this time of night?

Lovie starts toward the window, but I catch her

arm and drag her back. We can't risk showing ourselves until we're sure the naughty geriatrics have turned in for the night.

We wait five of the longest minutes in eternity, then hightail it toward the window and freedom.

"That was close." Lovie leans against the railing and the balcony lists like the bow of a ship in a heavy storm. "What are we going to do now, Callie?"

"Regroup."

It's raining harder. Most people would give up and go home, but not us. Lovie and I pride ourselves on being different. When everybody else is going left we go right.

My strong streak of independence (Jack calls it *stubbornness*) comes from Mama. She says people who always follow the crowd are *lemmings*—those little creatures who follow the herd over the cliffs and to their deaths rather than risk behavior that sets them apart.

The only thing Lovie and I have ever been traditional about is weddings and babies. We believe in church christenings and church weddings (for all the good that did me). But I'm sticking by my beliefs, no matter what.

I climb back into the tree and when Lovie joins me, it shakes like a twig in a monsoon. Grabbing the tree trunk, I hang on.

"Which window?" she asks. "Right or left?"

It's like asking which door hides the prizes.

Jack's in one, Bertha's in the other. Choose correctly and you get the prize. Choose wrong and you get the consequences. In this case, an almost-ex who may or may not be home . . . and in a forgiving, nonnosy mood.

"Let's use the scientific method and find out," I tell Lovie.

"You don't know, do you?"

"Holy cow! I'm in a *tree*."

"Well, so am I."

In a huff and getting soaked, I try to figure out how I can blame all this on Jack, but my generous nature prevails. Being up a tree is my own fault. I should have ignored the crime scene tape and minded my own business. I should have climbed into my bed with my two faithful doggie companions keeping watch and let the law handle murder.

"At least I'm not mooning half of Las Vegas," Lovies says, reminding me of our Bubbles Caper. We both laugh so hard we nearly fall out of our precarious perch.

Our good humor and resolve restored, Lovie starts saying, "Eenie, meanie," and I join in with "Minie, moe."

By clever deduction we pinpoint the window on our left as Bertha's, and I head that way. Sort of. Getting onto a slick balcony from a tree that is slightly off center presents logistical problems.

"Step on my branch, Lovie, and see if the tree

74

will lean far enough so I can get a foothold on the balcony."

"Why don't I just shimmy down the trunk, uproot the tree, and move it over three feet?"

"That would work."

"Smart-ass."

She stomps down on my limb and I fly through the air with the greatest of ease. If I didn't have the body of an athlete and the tenacity of Elvis insisting he's an international icon, I'd be flattened on the pavement. Instead, I grab the railing on the upswing and vault over the side on the downswing.

"You'd better stay in the tree, Lovie. I don't think you can make it."

Saying a word that jeopardizes her chances of prissing through the Pearly Gates, she gets on all fours and wobbles along the limb.

"Give me a hand, Callie."

While I try to maneuver her across five feet of empty space, I petition Mother Earth, Buddha, and the spirit of the late, great Karl Wallenda. Flying acrobat.

Getting Lovie onto the balcony will be a miracle on the order of the parting of the Red Sea. While I tug, Mother Nature provides the sounds effects. Crashing thunder and lightning bolts followed by a monsoon.

"Pull, Callie."

"I'm pulling."

We crash backward onto the balcony. If that

75

didn't wake Bertha, she's dead. Which would be just our luck.

Still, heedless of the deluge and the possibility of getting struck down before my eggs ever have a chance to be fertilized, I sit on the balcony and count my blessings.

"Am I alive?" Lovie asks.

"Yes, am I?"

"You bet your sweet patootie." Lovie stands up, wrings water out of her shirt, and puts on her gloves (another little trick she learned from "Slick Fingers" Johnson, the black-sheep cousin Jarvetis never claims). "As soon as we get in there and crack this case, I'm going out the front door. I don't care what Bertha's doing."

It turns out the new widow's asleep with a night-light glowing beside her bed and an open bottle of Valium on her night-stand. That would explain her sleeping through the noisiest breaking and entering since Fayrene set pots and pans at the entrance of Gas, Grits, and Guts to catch the lawless sportsman who was stealing her fish bait.

"I guess we don't have to be quiet." Leaving a trail of wet footprints on the baby-blue carpet that doesn't match another single thing in the room, Lovie stomps over to Bertha's dressing table and proceeds to sack and pillage.

Meanwhile, I grab the stack of mail on her bed-side table and check it by the night-light. You never know. Maybe Bertha's been corresponding with hit men.

There's nothing of interest here. Just an overdue light bill and a recent bill from Deb's Deep Discounts, a place that sells shoes I wouldn't be caught dead in. What did I expect from somebody with her lack of fashion sense?

"Look what we have here." Lovie tromps over and holds out a rhinestone hairpin. "See, it has the same daisy design as the one behind your tea olive."

If it's not an exact match it's close enough to fool me. And I'm an expert on fashion and beauty. Still . . .

"That's not proof she killed Dick. Or was hiding behind my tea olive."

"Yeah, but it's the only one on her dresser. Which means she lost the other one somewhere. It's evidence." Lovie pockets the hairpin.

"It's a start," I say. "Keep looking."

Bertha moans and we jump like the guilty. Peering over Lovie's shoulder, I hold my breath till she settles back into her pillows and resumes snoring.

She could use a good haircut. If I weren't in her apartment illegally, I'd leave a business card.

When I'm certain she's down for the count, I whisper to Lovie, "You search the drawers, I'll take the closet."

I don't know what I expect to find. I'm still new

at skullduggery. But since the Bubbles Caper, Lovie and I have started watching detective shows. TV killers keep evidence of their crimes—I guess to prove how powerful they are.

I can reach the top shelf of Bertha's closet without a step stool. The usual suspects are there—purses, scarves, gloves. I can tell you one thing: Bertha Gerard could use a personal shopper. Nothing matches. And it's all jumbled in a heap. I ram my arm under the untidy mess, reach as far back as I can, and pull out a small, spiral-bound book.

Kneeling beside the night-light, I realize I've just hit pay dirt. Keeping my voice low, I call Lovie.

She hurries over and squats beside me. "What is it?"

"Bertha's diary."

Thumbing through, I catch glimpses of her life. Trips to the dentist, fried green tomatoes at Romie's Grocery, a broken toe playing tennis. The daily minutia that makes up her life. I feel like a Peeping Tom.

I'm about to put it back when I see an entry that could crack this case wide open.

"Lovie, listen to this. *Jilted lovers who are jealous because I have Dick. Leonora M., Josie K., Lovie V.*"

"Let me see that." Lovie snatches the diary. "It's all a pack of lies. Leonara M. is bound to be Leonora Moffett, and she's never been jilted in her life. She does the ditching."

"Who do you think Josie K. is?"

"You remember Josephine Kessler who moved here from Memphis two years ago and stayed only four months?"

"The one with the bad bleach job?"

"That's the one. She had an affair with Dick, but she didn't give a flip about him."

"How do you know?"

"I catered her sister Abby's wedding reception. People talk."

Bertha gives a big snort and we freeze. She turns over, fumbles on the bedside table, and knocks off the plastic bottle of valium. It rolls across the carpet and lands at my feet. I see my future unfold—hairdresser to female prisoners.

If I get out of here without being arrested, I swear to Bloomingdale's I'll never play detective again.

Maybe that's going too far. My family might need me. I'll grab the evidence and run, that's what I'll do. I won't stand over somebody's bed and carry on a whole conversation.

Two lifetimes later Bertha gurgles, her hand flops off the table, and she settles back into heavy snoring. Somebody up there likes me.

Adding *stealing* to our growing list of crimes, Lovie pockets the diary with my hundred percent blessing. No sense leaving incriminating evidence behind even if it is a deliberate, calculated falsehood.

We tiptoe out of the bedroom and she nods toward the door.

"Car keys," I whisper, motioning her to go on. What I'm really thinking is *Jack*. It would be just like him to divine my presence and waylay me in the hall.

I wait till Lovie's out of the door before I climb through the window. Thank goodness, the monsoon has stopped. A few stars are even peeping out.

With every nerve I have shredded, I don't have enough resolve left to play Tarzan swinging through the jungle in a rainstorm. If I get off this balcony alive, I swear to give up sex.

But only with Jack.

I reach as far as my long arms will allow, grab the end of a branch, and pull it toward the balcony. Sending petitions to the god of second chances, I vault into the tree, then hang there, clinging to the trunk and trying to breathe.

What's that sound? I lean down as far as I dare, listening.

If somebody besides Lovie is under this tree, I'm up to my wet T-shirt in trouble.

Chapter 6

Fancy Footwork, Fancy Lying, and Double Trouble

I have two choices, shimmy down and face the music or wait him out. (Assuming there is somebody gunning for me under the tree.) If I wait, Lovie will come looking, and then she'll be the one dealing with the problem.

I'd shave my crowning glory before I'd do that to her. I start my descent. St. Peter ought to put a star by my name.

My foot slips on a wet limb but I remain cool. Translated: I don't wet my pants.

With feet and bladder finally under control, I inch downward. When I touch ground I consider bending down to kiss the earth.

In fact, I *do* bend down. But only to search for my car keys. Straining my eyes and sweeping my arms in long arcs, I come up empty. They can't be far. I distinctly heard them hit the ground.

I make another futile arc, then hear that noise again. In the mud on my knees, I whisper, "Lovie? Is that you?"

"Guess again."

Jack steps out of the shadows, and I don't know whether to slap him silly or fall into his arms in a relieved, ragged heap.

"I swear, Jack Jones. You scared me to death."

"Fancy meeting you here." He hauls me up and pulls me hard against his chest. "My, *my.* You're all wet."

His wicked lips make me forget my promise of abstinence. If he kisses me like that again I won't be responsible for getting arrested on public property for indecent exposure.

While I try to act as if don't want to wallow in the mud and make his babies, he's looking at me like he can't decide whether to spank me or have me for a midnight snack.

"Let me go, Jack Jones."

He laughs, but turns me loose, then leans against the tree. "Don't mind me. Go ahead with what you were doing." I stand there with my hands on my hips trying to outstare him. "What *were* you doing, Callie?"

"None of your business."

"In that case, I guess you don't need these." He pulls my keys out of his pocket and dangles them just out of my reach.

"What are you doing with my keys?"

"What are you doing up a tree in the middle of the night? Besides getting into trouble."

Mama taught me the best defense is a good offense. "Why are you still here? I thought you were headed to parts unknown."

"Not until I rescue you, Callie."

Good grief. He makes rescue sound like something risqué. And it probably is in the hands of Jack Jones.

"Give me the keys."

"First, promise you'll keep your pretty little nose out of this murder investigation."

"How did you know about that?" As if I have to ask. Jack's like the Shadow. Everywhere at once. Finding out stuff that only a Houdini could know.

Plus, Uncle Charlie or Mama could have told him. Both of them think my almost-ex is right up there with Lovie's Jack Daniel's apple pie and buttered rum ice cream.

"Say you'll let the authorities handle this, Cal."

Squared off with Jack, I guess I ought to feel proud of myself for not caving in. *Listen,* he's the kind of delicious man who can melt the strongest woman's resolve, and I never pretended to be one of those iron-willed, boardroom, ball-busting types. I like Passion Pink fingernail polish and Jungle Gardenia perfume as well as the next woman.

"You've lost the right to protect me, Jack."

His silence is so intense I swear I can hear a falling star. Just before I pop out of my skin, he reaches for my hand, presses the keys inside, then closes my fingers over them.

My heart stops. I swear it does.

And when he bends over and kisses my fist, I

channel Julie London singing "Cry Me a River." Men who are macho one minute and tender the next ought to be outlawed.

"Night, Cal. Take care."

I couldn't move if I were in the path of a herd of stampeding mustangs. When Lovie walks up, I jump two feet.

"I just saw Jack. What was that all about?"

"Don't ask."

I head to my Dodge Ram, keeping well ahead of her. A miracle considering I never outwalk or outrun Lovie.

By the time she gets to my truck, I have the engine running.

"Are you sure about this divorce, Callie?"

"How can anybody ever be sure about anything?" It's been a long day, and I'm not in the mood for introspection. "Lovie, what do you know about Bertha?"

"Same thing you do. She used to sell lingerie at Victoria's Secret, but I haven't seen her there in a while. She was pleasant enough but didn't go out of her way to help you."

"Do you think she's the killer?"

"I can see why she'd want to kill Dick. If Rocky did that to me, though, I'd choose something more creative, like tying him to the back of my van and dragging him over six miles of bad backcountry roads."

Lovie loves to shock.

"But why would she want to knock off Brian Watson?"

"I don't know, Callie. Maybe her diary will tell us something."

Stopped at a red light in the Elvis Presley District of east Tupelo, I mull over the things we know. Brian was a waiter, Dick a postman, and they lived in different states. But they were both thirty-something, good-looking Elvis impersonators trying to be named the best tribute artist at the festival.

The more I think about this angle, the more I'm convinced I'm on the right track. All the impersonators have motive and opportunity. As far as I know, Bertha was nowhere near the Birthplace when Brian died.

"Lovie, what if one of the other impersonators is trying to kill the competition?"

"I'll help him."

"The singing wasn't that bad."

"Ask your dog. He'll back me up."

"Be serious, Lovie. I think we're on to something."

"You be serious if you want to. It's after midnight. All I want is to brush my teeth and go to bed."

By the time we get back to Mooreville, the sky is clear— which bodes well for tomorrow's festival activities—and the stars are out in force. I park the Dodge Ram and we sprint into the house, then strip off our damp clothes and put on pajamas. Black silk and lace from an expensive bridal lingerie shop in Memphis for Lovie—what else?—and Walmart Betty Boops for me.

In the bathroom she says, "I forgot my toothbrush," and I tell her, "You can borrow mine."

With that, we haul off to bed without even saying good night, Lovie in my guest room painted the color of sunshine and me in my big cushy bed with my faithful doggie sentinels on either side.

Hoyt is chasing a rabbit in his dreams, his little legs jerking. Judging by the sound of Elvis smacking his lips, he's dreaming of fried peanut butter and banana sandwiches, the King's signature dish and a favorite treat for my basset. Content, I burrow into my pillow and watch the stars through the skylight.

Sometimes, all it takes to make you feel good is knowing people (and pets) you love are nearby.

The next morning Lovie and I have breakfast al fresco. The Angel Garden is usually my spot of choice, but crime tape spoils the ambience, so we opt for the front porch.

Lovie has cooked pecan waffles and bacon. She thinks it's bad luck to start the day with a stingy breakfast. If you do, she claims, everything else coming your way that day will be puny.

I can go along with that. My own beliefs are so far off the beaten path I'd be barred from singing duets with Lovie at Wildwood Baptist Church if they knew.

Over waffles Lovie says she's leaving Bertha's diary with me. "Between cooking for the Elvis Festival and getting ready for Rocky, I don't have time to read it."

"Okay. I'll take a look as soon as I can." I don't know when. I've got to get to Hair.Net this morning to take care of my business.

After breakfast, I put on a CD of Native American flute music, then burn sacred white sage for good measure, fanning the smoke around us with the redtail hawk feather I bought last September at the White Buffalo Powwow in Tupelo. If there are any bad spirits lingering around after Dick's murder, I'm sending them on the run.

I inherited more than olive skin and high cheekbones from my dearly departed daddy, Michael Valentine: I got enough Cherokee blood that ancient Native American beliefs and rituals resonate with me.

Lovie and I do the dishes and then she heads to the festival. After I dress Elvis in his pink bow tie and myself in a blue sundress with matching Burberry ballerina flats, we make a detour by my beauty shop.

The impersonators won't need me until this afternoon right before their competition starts. On the other hand, my regulars count on me to make them feel gorgeous.

Listen, if a woman's hair looks good, she feels good all over. I built my reputation by making sure my clients have the best-looking hair in Lee County.

Bitsy Morgan is waiting for me, all ears to hear what I have to say about the murder in Mooreville. The community grapevine is the best I've ever seen, mainly because Fayrene makes it her business to tell everything she knows. Ask anybody in Mooreville. If you want gossip with your gas, all you have to do is walk into Gas, Grits, and Guts and says, "Hey, Fayrene, what's new?"

I'm not above doing it, myself. I like a good story as well as the next person as long as it's not mean and doesn't hurt anybody.

While I transform Bitsy from gray to medium blond, I tell her the bare details, leaving Lovie out of it.

That satisfies her and she moves on to her bursitis and her nephew's new job in Memphis.

Mama pops by and proceeds to plop down at my manicure table and paint her nails a hot pink that clashes with her tunic. I'd steer her toward peach if I weren't still outdone with her about dirty dancing with Texas Elvis.

"I'm thinking of getting a cowboy hat," she says.

"Whatever for, Mama?" If she says *a little trip to Texas,* I'm calling Uncle Charlie.

"Fayrene and I are going two-stepping over in Tunica." Home of genuine Vegas casinos built right in the middle of Mississippi cotton fields. Listen, I'd rather have the cotton.

But I'm so relieved Mama's not hauling off to Texas I don't even get upset when she calls me into my office and asks for fifty dollars. She calls it a *little loan;* I call it a donation. Some people would say I'm supporting her vices, but I prefer to look at it as subsidizing Mama's happiness. What's the harm in a bit of gambling if it makes her forget all the years she spent raising a daughter alone and never looking at another man because nobody could hold a candle to Michael Valentine?

What can I say? Mama has five card stud; I have designer shoes.

By the time I get to Tupelo, it's after twelve. Terry Matthews, G. I. Elvis from Pensacola, is waiting in my hairdressing tent. He's a chemist and a dead ringer for the King. In army uniform, he's the only one not wearing a spangled bell-bottom jumpsuit. I've heard he sings so much like his idol you almost believe they buried somebody else in Graceland and Elvis still lives.

I'm pulling for him.

"Good morning, Terry." I stow my purse under the table while my dog starts nosing around for crumbs. Like I didn't just feed him enough to sustain a small third-world country. "I hope you haven't been waiting long."

I don't make appointments at the festival. The hair station is here strictly as a courtesy.

"Thirty minutes." As if his tone weren't haughty enough, G. I. Elvis checks his watch to be sure.

Major mistake. My dog comes over and slimes the leg of his pants. G. I. Elvis streaks out, leaving the scent of cheap pomade.

I've changed my mind about who ought to win and who ought to lose. When we get home I'm giving Elvis a steak.

Since nobody else is waiting for my deft touch, I put my clever basset back on his leash, then stroll to the refreshment booth.

Beulah Jane is in a dither. With cheeks flushed and hair awry, she appears to be suffering from stress overload.

"Lord, Callie. I'm so glad to see you I could die." This is a big turnaround from yesterday when she was jockeying to be in charge of the tour, but I give her the benefit of the doubt. Tragedy sometimes brings out the best in people.

Beulah Jane pours two glasses of peach tea, hands one to me, then turns the sign on the booth to CLOSED.

"Thanks." The tea is just what I need. I'm hot all over from G. I. Elvis' rebuke, not to mention the ninety-degree weather. Remembering the fit Beulah Jane had over my dog riding the bus, I ask her, "You don't mind if Elvis comes in?"

"I'm so upset a brass band could come in and I wouldn't care."

"What's wrong?"

"The Tupelo police were waiting for us this morning. Now that Dick's dead, Brian's death has been ruled *homicide*."

"Was Lovie here?"

"Lord, yes. They grilled her like she was a pure dee criminal. Then proceeded to turn our food supply upside down taking samples. It was a disgrace."

"Where is she now?"

"She said she was headed home. The way they were trying to pin Brian Watson's death on her, I don't blame her."

"She didn't even know him before this festival."

"That's what Lovie told them, but I don't think they believed her. And her, a fine upstanding citizen. Of all the nerve!"

"Did she say she was coming back?"

"No. I told her the fan club officers could take care of the booth. No need for her to stay here and put up with that kind of harassment. Not to mention the stares."

"What stares?"

"Oh, you know. Word gets around."

I'm so mad I'd like to slap somebody. Just about anybody would do.

But my good southern upbringing prevails. I thank Beulah Jane profusely (she's the kind of woman who thrives on praise), then head to the T-shirt booth. The tribute artists will just have to make do with their own hair gel.

With Lovie on the hot seat for two murders, it's time for another family summit.

Elvis' Opinion #4 on Appearances, Suspects, and Gossip

If Callie would let me off this leash I could nose around the festival for suspects and gossips.

And maybe keep an eye peeled for a foxy Lhasa apso or a sassy Pomeranian. Don't get me wrong. Ann-Margret (my hot-to-trot French poodle) is the only one I'm crooning "I'm Yours" to, but I'd be a lesser dog if I didn't check out my options.

Looking at my debonair exterior, you might think I'm nothing more than a sex symbol and a pretty face, but I'm a dog of many talents. If my human mom would turn me loose I could rout out the gossipmongers and teach them a lesson before you could say "Don't Step on My Blue Suede Shoes."

Nobody talks bad about a Valentine and escapes my wrath. Usually I'm the nonviolent type, but if Charlie hadn't come along a few weeks ago when I was sporting on the farm with my little Frenchie, I'd have gnawed the leg off that sleazy character who wanted to spread gossip about Ruby Nell.

It wouldn't take me long to find who's spreading lies about Lovie. I can smell the stench of mendacity a mile. (Listen, I'm no intellectual slouch. I know Tennessee Williams as well as that prissy shihtzu who lives down the street. He thinks he's hot stuff because he can quote whole scenes from *Cat on a Hot Tin Roof.* Well, I've got news for him. Put me center stage under some hot lights and I could do a Brick that would make Paul Newman jealous.)

As for finding the suspects, I have my theories. Plus, of course, my keen hearing. Why do you think God gave me mismatched ears? Because I'm smarter than the average dog, that's why. Take a cocker spaniel, for instance. Hoyt wouldn't have the slightest idea what to do with information gleaned from judicious eavesdropping. But I just soak it all up, bide my time, and wait for the right moment to reveal myself as a star canine investigator.

I guess that's one of the reasons I got sent back as a dog. With my performing experience and people skills, not to mention my big heart and generous nature, I am the perfect addition to the Valentine family.

There's no such thing as coincidence. Everything in life is part of a big plan. And I'm the foundation of the Valentine plan. Bereavement counselor at Charlie's funeral home; protector, confidant, comforter, and oracle of wisdom for Callie; cheerleader for the entire family and doggie detective when the need arises. (Lately, it's arising with a regularity that would be depressing if they didn't have me around for entertainment value and bragging rights.)

A lesser dog couldn't juggle all these roles, but I'm the King. I can do anything.

Right now, I'm helping Callie keep up appearances. Who better to enhance the Valentine family reputation than a show dog who can wag his tail with the best of the pedigreed (and even the unpedigreed riffraff) and still look intelligent and sophisticated?

Chapter 7

Character Flaws, Dirty Linen, and Swiveling Hips

As Elvis and I weave through the festival crowd, it's obvious word has gotten around about the two dead impersonators. In spite of the carnival atmosphere—hot dogs, balloons, souvenir T-shirts, plus the rocking piano and whiskey-voiced vocals of the Mississippi Delta blues great Eden Brent—people are acting skittish. They're peering over their shoulders and cutting their eyes around to see who's behind them.

Even I'm not normal. Usually I don't have a paranoid bone in my body, but today I imagine everybody is staring at me and talking. *Did you know her house is a crime scene? Did you know her cousin is suspected of murder?*

I must have some heretofore hidden character flaw. When I get home (if I ever do) I'm going to light white candles under the moon, repent of falling off the abstinence wagon with Jack, and petition Mother Earth to make me a better person.

But first I have to find Lovie and catch a killer. Oh, and did I mention *make sure Love Me Tender Elvis from Tennessee ditches his awful wig before this afternoon's competition?* It looks like a dead guinea pig on his head. If he gets onstage wearing that ill-fitting, moth-eaten rug, Elvis is likely to drag it off his head and give it a decent burial. Not to mention that my reputation as Lee County's premiere stylist will be ruined.

Trotting toward the T-shirt booth as fast as Elvis can keep up, I whip out my cell phone.

"Lovie, where are you?"

"In my kitchen beheading shrimp and mutilating tomatoes."

"You're making jambalaya?"

"Yes, and garlic mashed potatoes, cheese grits, black-eyed peas, whiskey-glazed carrots, jalapeño corn bread, brandied peaches, and chocolate cherry cake."

"Holy cow, Lovie. Are you making all that for Rocky?"

"No. For me. I'm not about to go to prison hungry."

"You're not going to prison. I'm headed to the T-shirt booth to talk with Uncle Charlie and Mama. How fast can you get down here?"

"I've removed myself from the lynch mob. I'm not coming back."

"You're innocent, Lovie, and we're going to act that way. Besides, we need to come up with a plan to find the real killer."

I guess I must be doing something right because she promises to stow the food, clean the fishy smell off her hands with lemon, and come back, pronto. And I don't even have to bribe her.

Obviously, murder has unhinged her. Lovie usually drives a harder bargain. There was that time I wanted her to back up the tiny little fib I told Jack, and it cost my favorite pair of Juicy Couture sandals.

Well, the fib wasn't exactly tiny. It all happened last year at Thanksgiving just a few weeks before he left me. We'd been going back and forth about having children and I told him I was pregnant. My intentions were good. I thought if I could get him excited about the prospect of a fictional baby, I'd have no trouble nudging him into having a real one.

It all backfired. I lied, Lovie lied, and we fooled Jack for all of two minutes. All because of a small error: I forgot I always get this twitch in my eye when I'm not telling the absolute, unvarnished truth. I don't know why I thought I could get by with such a whopper. Listen, I can't even successfully tell a little white lie.

I'm glad the cops didn't question me. I'd probably have confessed last night's breaking and entering along with stealing (the diary) and withholding evidence (both the diary and the rhinestone pin).

Mama sees me coming and waves. When I see her clashing fingernail polish in the bright light of day I repent my earlier decision not to steer her away from her fashion faux pas. Okay, so she won't receive stars in her crown for motherhood, but she's my biggest fan and defender. If I'd been the one in the kitchen questioned for murder, she'd have been in there taking names and kicking butt.

"Hey, Mama." I lean down to kiss her cheek, and she says, "What's that all about?"

"Nothing. Just because." I hug Uncle Charlie, then settle into the red canvas camp chair beside Mama and unsnap Elvis' leash.

He makes a beeline for Uncle Charlie, whom he adores. Mainly, I think because Uncle Charlie's the closest thing I know to a guardian angel on this earth, but also because he sometimes takes my dog fishing and lets Elvis sample the fish bait.

He bends down to scratch Elvis' ears. "I was going to call you, dear heart. You heard about Lovie?"

"Beulah Jane told me they grilled her and took food samples. I wonder what they're looking for."

"The detectives are waiting on toxicology reports. If Jack were here we'd know more."

Uncle Charlie thinks Jack can turn water to wine. Well, sure, they fish together and tell the same jokes and get along like father and son, but I don't see how that translates into Jack being the answer to all our prayers.

Someday I'm going to ask Uncle Charlie why, but now is not the time.

"We don't need Jack," I tell him, and Mama gives me this *look* like she's the queen of some small country and I've committed high treason and might get my head chopped off. "We just need to find out who did it. And fast."

"Here comes Fayrene." Mama motions her friend to the white camp chair. "Maybe she can help."

Dressed in lime-green slacks and blouse, Fayrene looks like a cucumber. I mean that in the best way. Cucumbers are a personal favorite of mine.

"Whatever it is, of *course* I can help. I have ESPN." Fayrene plops down beside Mama. "I don't even need a weatherman to tell me when the barium pressure is high. I can tell just by my ultra-sensory precipitations."

"Great," Mama tells her. "You got your dancing shoes?"

"Right here." Fayrene pats a purse the size of the Grand Canyon, then jerks her mirror out and fluffs up her hair. "I swear, Jarvetis was so mad this morning I couldn't half pimp."

Translation: primp. And what in the world was Jarvetis mad about? Surely not the dancing. He's the mildest-mannered man I know. He didn't even get angry when Fayrene sold his favorite bird dog in a fit of revenge over his adding pickled pig's lips to the inventory without consulting her. She thought nobody would buy them, and they've turned out to be her next to highest-selling item, running a close second to boiled peanuts.

I remind myself to ask Mama. Jarvetis and

Fayrene are Mooreville's Desi and Lucy, Bogart and Bacall, George and Gracie— so famous as a couple I can't imagine Gas, Grits, and Guts with only one of them.

Lovie arrives with a basket of food and proceeds to serve hunks of chocolate cherry cake, her favorite remedy for trouble, guaranteed to take your mind off everything except murder.

The crowd has thinned because of the heat, and nobody's near the T-shirt booth. It's the perfect time to discuss our private investigation.

I put my half-eaten cake aside and look straight at Fayrene, Mooreville's Mouth. Which is the unmitigated truth, no matter how much I like her. "Everything that's said in this booth stays in the booth."

"Cross my heart and hope to outlive Jarvetis," she says.

Things at Gas, Grits, and Guts must be worse than I thought.

"Lovie, did you bring the rhinestone hairpins?" I ask.

She pulls them out of her pocket while I tell where we found them, leaving out the part about the first one being behind the tea olive instead of the Confederate jasmine. I don't want to hurt Fayrene's feelings.

The great thing about loyal family and friends is you don't have to explain things, like why you didn't turn evidence over to the cops.

"I knew I saw Bertha behind that bush," Fayrene says.

"This is still not proof she killed Dick," I say. "It's a common type you can buy at Walmart. Anybody at the party could have lost it."

"I have one just like it," Lovie says, which is news to me. Bad news, and all the more reason I'm glad we withheld evidence. "I discovered it this morning when I was rambling through my bathroom drawers looking for a ponytail holder."

"You have a set?" Mama asks.

"No. I guess I lost one. I have no idea where."

Even worse.

"Oh, pshaw!" Fayrene waves her hand about. "Anybody can be forgetful. The last time I was in Walmart I forgot to buy Jarvetis' expositories. And him not even able to sit without a cushion."

If I don't do something fast, this summit is going to turn from murder to hemorrhoids. I lead the discussion back to Bertha's motive, but nobody has a clue why she would kill Dick *and* Brian.

When Lovie repeats my theory that one of the impersonators is knocking off the competition, Fayrene jumps right in.

"I'll bet it was George Blakely."

Otherwise known as Texas Elvis.

"You're just jealous because he danced with me and not you." Mama in a huff is a sight to behold—eyes and cheeks blazing. And I swear even her hair springs up like the tines on a devil's pitchfork.

"Mama, have you had the scissors to your hair?"

"Why do you ask?" She fluffs it, a sure sign of guilt.

"You have."

"Only to trim a little straggle or two."

I don't leave straggles and Mama knows it. Just wait till she asks me for another fifty dollars. I'm likely to give her only thirty.

"Dear hearts, let's get back to George. Fayrene, why do you think he might have killed Dick and Brian?"

"Because I heard him in an argument with Dick about who was going to win the tribute artist competition."

"When was this?" Uncle Charlie asks.

"Last night at the party. Right after the impersonators got there."

"Do you recall exactly what George said?" I ask.

"Naturally. He said *I'm going to win this contest no matter what it takes.*"

Mama jumps to his defense. "George is a bit arrogant and high strung, but I don't think he's a murderer. What about that one from Tennessee? He has shifty eyes."

"Love Me Tender Elvis is a pussycat," I say. "I guarantee his only crime is bad hair."

"You don't know that, Carolina." When Mama gets really upset with me she calls me by my full name, which I hate. It makes me feel like a state. Though I guess I'm lucky she didn't name me

103

Georgia and call me George. "Any one of the impersonators had the same motive and opportunity."

"Still, Mama . . . he may be the best lead we have."

Uncle Charlie steps in. "Why don't you and Lovie follow that lead while I research the Internet to see what I can find out about our impersonators? Ruby Nell, can you and Fayrene handle the T-shirt booth till I get back?"

"As long as you're back by four, Charlie."

For reasons I can't fathom, Uncle Charlie is not too happy with Mama's demand. Usually he's Mama's staunchest supporter and defender, no matter how outrageous she acts.

Is he rattled because he needs to be at Eternal Rest taking care of business, or could it be he doesn't like Mama's latest venture? If he's upset about something as innocuous as dancing, he must have a good reason.

I'll have to keep an eye on the situation . . . as soon as I have a free eye to use. Between murder of the impersonators and my dog custody suit with Jack, I'm lucky to keep up with my own business, much less Mama's.

Putting Elvis back on his leash, Lovie and I set out to uncover Texas Elvis' dirty linen. But first we detour by my hairstyling tent so I can get the impersonators ready for the mid-afternoon round of competition.

There's only one tribute artist waiting, and thank goodness it's Love Me Tender Elvis. His real name is Thaxton Miller, a handsome thirty-something salesman at a motorcycle shop in Memphis. Festival scuttlebutt is that the spirit of Graceland has rubbed off on him and he's a shoo-in to win.

I don't know whether he channels Elvis or not. I haven't heard him sing. All I know is that I'm fixing to make Thaxton's hair look so good you'd have to be Elvis' mama to tell it from the real thing.

Removing the guinea pig wig from his head, I say, "Do you want me to dispose of this?"

"No. I'm keeping it for sentimental reasons."

I don't know how anybody can be sentimental about a hairpiece that looks like roadkill, but I'm too polite to ask.

Lovie winks at me and pulls a chair close to Thaxton. "Do you enter these competitions often?"

"Every chance I get."

"Then you must know a lot of the other tribute artists."

I see where she's going with these questions, and I'm happy to leave the interrogation to Lovie. When I'm in the middle of hair, I like to use every ounce of concentration on making it look wonderful. That's why people call me a hair artist instead of a mere stylist.

When she asks about Texas Elvis, Thaxton says, "Yeah, I know George. We play cards together."

"Then you know him pretty well."

"Naw. It's just an occasional card game. All I know is he likes cigars and Miller Lite."

Not a very good case for murder.

Before Lovie can ask more, I've finished transforming Love Me Tender Elvis and he's sprinting toward the stage saying he can't be late for the competition.

"What was his big hurry?" Lovie says.

"Guilt?"

"I don't know. Maybe we're barking up the wrong tree with George."

"Right now, it's the best tree we have. Come on, Lovie."

By the time I've put the CLOSED sign on the tent flap, the competition is under way again and fans are going wild. As Lovie and I press through the crowd, she grabs my arm.

"Somebody's following us."

"Good grief, Lovie. In this madhouse, how can you tell?"

"As Fayrene would say, *it's my ESPN*."

Lovie jokes even when she's scared to death, and to tell the truth, I'm not feeling so brave myself. In light of recent events I'm glad Elvis is with us, even if he's never had to prove himself as a watchdog.

Chapter 8

Gamblin', Lyin', and Cheatin'

Jack once told me petty criminals target weak people, that if I ever think I'm being followed I should act like a woman nobody in his right mind would mess with. Naturally, I said, *I am*, which veered us onto a different path I don't care to remember. It's ninety-four degrees and I'm hot enough already.

"Lovie, on the count of three, turn around and act like you're going to beat the tar out of somebody."

She doesn't ask why (a tribute to the kind of friendship we have). I start counting and when I get to three we whirl around. Nobody I know is behind us except Beulah Jane.

"Mercy." She puts her hand over her heart. "You scared me to death."

"Sorry," I said. "We just passed the lemonade vendor and I'm about to parch."

"If you don't want lemonade, Tewanda just made a fresh batch of peach tea. I would've stayed to help her, but my bladder's about to pop." Beulah Jane heads toward the portable potties, then backtracks. "Are you all right, Lovie? I thought you went home."

"I decided nobody's going to intimidate me."

"Well, law, if I had that kind of spunk I'd be president of the Garden Club."

As Beulah Jane tootles off toward the toilets, Lovie and I grab a lemonade.

"I told you nobody was following us, Lovie."

"Don't be too sure. I saw Bertha ducking behind the corn dog vendor."

We take off in that direction, but if Bertha really did leave off mourning dead Dick long enough to partake of the Elvis festivities, she's blended back into the crowd, an easy thing to do since this year's attendance has set a record—eleven thousand people.

As Love Me Tender Elvis croons his ballad, the younger fans jam the blocked-off streets around the portable stage, screaming and throwing scarves. Veteran festival goers have moved their lawn chairs to the few bits of shade downtown Tupelo offers—the east side of Tupelo Hardware, the little park east of Reed's Department Store, the Alley across from the historic courthouse where wrought-iron tables are set up with umbrellas, and the sparse shade of crape myrtle trees Tupelo's beautification committee planted along Main Street and a few of its arteries.

Lovie's asking, "Which way now?" when my cell phone rings. It's Uncle Charlie.

"I think we're on the right track, Callie," he says. "There are photos on George's Web site of him with both Brian and Dick."

"Could they just be three impersonators posing for the camera?"

"No. These are candid shots. Looks like they're in the middle of a card game."

"Is Thaxton Miller in them, too?"

"Who?"

"Love Me Tender Elvis. From Memphis. You know . . . the one with the baby-blue bell-bottom jumpsuit and the rhinestone belt with TCB and the lightning bolt."

"No," Uncle Charlie says. "But Bertha's in the pictures."

"With Dick?"

"No. With George. And they look cozy. I'm going to keep digging."

After I hang up I tell Lovie the latest developments.

"Maybe George was messing around with Bertha," she says. "Have you had a chance to read any more of her diary?"

"Not yet. But now we have motives for both George and Bertha. Either one of them could have killed Dick to get him out of the way."

"Why would either of them kill Brian?"

"That's what we have to find out. This way, Lovie."

"Where?"

"You see that baby-blue jumpsuit? Thaxton Miller just finished his performance, and I intend to find out what he knows."

We catch up with him just as he finishes auto-graphing the program from a teenaged girl dressed mostly in freckles. I swear, if her cutoff blue jean shorts ride up any higher she'll be showing off Christmas (one of Grandmother Valentine's many euphemisms for private body parts).

Thaxton Miller is not too happy to see us, but since he knows we're both working this festival, he's too savvy to be rude. You never know who might have some influence with the judges.

"You did a great job onstage," I say, meaning it. "Lovie, get him a glass of iced peach tea, then meet us in the Alley."

It's a miniature courtyard across the street from the historic courthouse in what was once a junky alley between a row of upscale law offices and the Stables, a popular pub and restaurant. While Lovie heads toward the refreshment booth, I lead Love Me Tender Elvis toward an umbrella-shaded table beside a heat-distressed potted geranium.

"Thanks." Thaxton flops into the chair across from me. "But I'll never hold a candle to the King."

Judging by the way Elvis licks Thaxton's feet, I'd say my dog agrees. Or else, Thaxton has dropped ice cream on his boots.

Usually I'm a model of southern manners, but today I don't have time to sit around and make polite small talk. Lovie's future hinges on an expeditious apprehension of the real killer.

When she slides into the chair beside me with three glasses of tea and a paper cup of water for my basset, I say, "Thaxton, when you played cards with Geroge, were Dick and Brian the other part of the foursome?"

He looks like he'd rather be anywhere except with me discussing two dead Elvises. Still, I sense he's also rattled about something. If George has already killed two of his card-playing buddies, could it be that Thaxton is afraid he'll be next?

"They were," is all he says, and I can tell he's going to make me work for every little bit of information I get.

If I don't think of a way around this stalemate, this interrogation could take all day. While I'm discarding schemes as fast as I can dream them up, Lovie says, "George was boffing Dick's wife."

Thaxton's face turns a deep shade of red, but Lovie barrels forward as if she doesn't even notice. "Were you aware of that?"

"Bertha would never do that."

Holy cow. He sounds so angry I lean back in my chair to put some space between us. Thaxton Miller suddenly looks more like a suspect than the next victim.

What nerve did we touch? And how does he know what Bertha would do? Even more to the point, why would he defend her?

"Do the four of you still play cards?" I ask.

"No."

Could he be any more terse? What nerve did I hit now?

"Why not?" Lovie asks, and for a minute I think Thaxton is going to turn tail and run.

"Nobody wants to get in a game with somebody who cheats at cards."

"Who was cheating?" I ask.

"Dick." That figures. "George found out and called his hand."

"Did George have any issues with Brian?" Lovie asks.

"Not that I know of." Thaxton leans toward her. "Are you two with the cops or something?"

"No. Just gathering information for Daddy. He's on the festival committee, you know."

Lovie's a smooth liar. I used to think it was a character flaw, but ever since we landed up to our eyeballs in murder (the Bubbles Caper) I've begun to see her talent for prevarication as an asset.

Love Me Tender Elvis does an about-face and turns on the Tennessee charm, not to mention the drawl.

"I hope ya'll don't think I had anything to do with Dick's death."

Winking at him, Lovie says, "I'll be sure to tell Daddy how cooperative you were."

After Thaxton leaves we finish our peach tea and try to thrash the wheat from the chaff.

"He could have been lying," I say.

"About what?"

"Everything."

"I don't think so. How could he fake that reaction when I mentioned George and Bertha?"

"It could have been the way you said it, Lovie."

"Never underestimate shock value." She finishes her tea, then digs an ice cube out and starts sucking on it. "Assuming Thaxton told the truth, then George had double motive for killing Dick."

"That's two big *ifs*. *If* he was serious about Bertha and *if* he would kill over a deck of cards."

"John Wayne would."

"You've been watching too many old westerns, Lovie."

"My social life stinks."

"Rocky will take care of that when he gets here."

"That's not what I want him to take care of."

If Lovie gets on the holy grail again I don't know what I'm going to do. Fortunately my cell phone saves us all. It's Uncle Charlie again.

"I'm back at the T-shirt booth, dear heart, and I need to see you and Lovie. Right away."

"What's up?"

"I'll tell you as soon as you get here."

It's not like Uncle Charlie to be mysterious. I have a bad feeling about this.

Elvis' Opinion #5 on Style, Performance, and Top Billing

So far Thaxton Miller is the only contestant who can sing well enough to be worthy of wearing my sequined jumpsuit. But music aside, he was lying through his teeth to Callie and Lovie. If they'd let me off this leash I'd catch up to him and make him tell the truth.

Don't let this pretty face fool you. My early pals weren't called the Memphis Mafia for nothing.

And speaking of the good old days, every time I look across at what used to be the old Mississippi/Alabama fairgrounds and see how they tore down the grandstand, I want to march down to City Hall and jerk a knot in some tails. Reporters came all the way from London to cover my second—and final—concert there (1957). Never mind that I was at the bottom of the play-bill—behind the beef show, the 4-H Club style show, and the so-called *Daring Balloon Ascension and Jump.* My name was bigger and in bold print. Which is more than I can say for any of these upstarts at the festival today.

They think a tight spangled jumpsuit makes them Elvis. Don't get me wrong. It's flattering to have people imitating me after all these years. Back when I was rocking and rolling all over the world, I was the only entertainer wearing spangled costumes. Except Liberace. Not to knock his talent —but he wasn't in my league. He looked just plain over-the-top.

I had style. Still do.

Didn't care a whit (and still don't) that pink was considered sissy and no man in his right mind would put on a velvet shirt and stand up in front of a hometown crowd of people just like my folks—sharecroppers, small-time farmers, factory laborers, and dirt-poor kids who picked cotton so they'd have enough money for the gate fee.

I never did let fame go to my head, and still don't. I'll admit I put on the King bit in front of Ann-Margret, but it takes talent to lure a French poodle in heat away from the rest of the pack.

Speaking of which, I could give that feisty-looking beagle exuding pheromones over by the lemonade stand a run for her money if Callie would give me free rein at this festival. Not that I'd do anything serious like singing "Love Me," but I wouldn't mind humming a few bars of "Bosa Nova Baby."

Naturally we whiz on by so all I have time for is a wink and a wiggle, but Beagle Baby gets the point. She sets up a howl that causes her owner, a self-important matronly type, to hustle her off saying, "Now, stop that Fluffy."

"Great Balls of Fire"—to borrow from the piano-stomping Jerry Lee Lewis—if I'd been saddled with a name that silly I'd be howling myself. In outrage, not a song.

Instead I perk up my mismatched ears to see what's cooking over at the T-shirt booth. Charlie's on the phone. To Jack. Who is up to his own ears in trouble. *Big* trouble.

Callie's not going to be happy. I'd hate to be the one to tell her. I don't know how Charlie's going to break the news.

If I were in his shoes, I'd start with that gaudy bouquet of red roses. Which he does. Only it turns out they're not for Callie; they're for Lovie.

"For me?" She's as surprised as the rest of us. "Two dozen of them?"

Like me, Lovie gets around but not with the kind of lover who sends roses. If you ask me, it's about time somebody recognized her worth. I do what I can to teach her the value of herself, but as you know, I've got my hands full with my human mom.

Lovie looks at the card. "Rocky!"

"He wired them," Charlie says. "I guess he knew you'd be working the festival."

"I can't believe it." She buries her face in the flowers, and at the rate she's breathing on them, they'll be wilted within the hour. "Red means love eternal. Right, Callie?"

"I'd say it's a very good sign."

I've never been prouder of my human mom. She knows good and well red roses don't mean a darned thing except the man who sent them had money in his pocket and a yen for an extravagant gesture.

Last Christmas, Jack filled Callie's house with red roses. Must have cost him a small fortune. Every room smelled like Charlie's funeral home. And maybe that was the point. The death of a marriage. It sure as heck didn't mean love everlasting because he left the next day.

Not that I'm placing blame. Jack's human, just like the rest of us. (Well, I *used* to be and I still remember what it's like. If you ask me, dogs are a more evolved species, but sometimes I miss the emotional ups and downs of being like the rest of the unevolved, all that gut-busting joy and angst.)

I sidle up to Lovie and let her know how happy I am she got roses.

"Aren't they *great,* Elvis?" She leans down to pat me and I howl a few bars of "My Happiness," that little song I recorded so long ago for my mother, Gladys, at Sun Studios in Memphis.

Who knows? If I get lucky, Lovie will reward my loyalty and compassion by sneaking me a bite of that chocolate cake while Callie's not looking. Forget that dogs aren't supposed to have chocolate. Anybody worth his salt knows I'm a world-famous idol in dog's clothing.

117

Chapter 9

Dangerous George, Pee-Wee Herman, and Hot Air

I'm glad Lovie got roses. Really, I am. But I don't think that's why Uncle Charlie called us to come back to the T-shirt booth.

Mama and Fayrene are still here, fizzing around admiring the roses and changing out of Nikes and into dance shoes, Mary Jane pumps with low heels. Jazz shoes, we used to call them when Lovie and I were in our teens and taking dance lessons from Miss Bea Perkins, whose husband, Jim, walked out the door one morning and never came back. She lived in a white antebellum house on Church Street and kept Jim's slippers and robe on the chair beside the piano in the dance studio where he'd left them.

A performer by nature, Lovie soaked up dance, but I spent most of my time trying to blend in with the furniture so I'd get put on the back row where nobody would notice how gawky I was. In those dreaded spring recitals, Lovie always got to be a rose or a star and wear a pretty costume, while I was usually a tree or a turnip hidden behind fake leaves.

"Where's my comb? Where's my lipstick?" Mama's digging through her purse asking rhetorical questions, so I plop down in a camp chair to stay out of the hubbub and remember my own dancing days.

I didn't learn tap and ballet from Miss Bea, but I did learn that the heart beats on, no matter how empty the house is, that if you smile a lot and spend kindness like it's oil and you're a rich Texan, you fill up from the inside. And before you know it, the hole inside you is hidden under a crust so thick you barely even notice it's still there.

"Fayrene, are you about ready to go?" Mama blots her newly painted lips on a Kleenex and hangs her purse over her arm.

She's so one-sided about George Blakely I consider not even telling her what we learned before she leaves, but since the point is to help Lovie, I relent, summing it all up with "It looks like George Blakely had plenty of motive for killing Dick. I just don't see any reason he'd go after Brian."

"Well, I do," Fayrene pipes up, and I say, "My goodness. I didn't know you were playing detective, too."

"I've just made my debutt." *Debut,* I hope, though with Fayrene, you never can tell. "I can tell you exactly why George Blakely would kill Brian Watson. He was messing around with Brian's girlfriend."

"You don't know that for sure, Fayrene." It looks like Mama's going to her grave defending Texas Elvis.

"Well, I guess I do, Ruby Nell. My information came straight from the horse's ass."

I don't ask who the horse was, and I particularly don't want to know that part of his anatomy. Besides, I think Fayrene meant *mouth*.

Lovie's laughing so hard nobody can hear himself think, let alone talk. Finally she ceases guffawing long enough to make a sane comment.

"You're telling me somebody who looks like Pee-Wee Herman can get any woman he wants?"

"It's his hot air balloon," Fayrene says. "He hauls it to every competition just to get women. Apparently they love to take flight and check out George's rigging."

"He'd have to have more than a hot air balloon to make me want to check out his equipment," Lovie says, never mind that Uncle Charlie is standing right there.

"Now, now, dear heart," is all he says. He's such a gentleman.

"Well, I happen to think you're all barking up the wrong tree." Mama actually sniffs when she's in a snit. "Personally, I think George wouldn't hurt a flea. And for your information, he bears a remarkable resemblance to George Clooney." She jerks up her purse. "Fayrene, are you going to stand there all day and report falsehoods or are you coming with me?"

"Not if you don't get off your high horse."

They march out arm in arm, though it appears to

120

me Mama's still on her horse. That arrogant tilt to her head and the way she's prissing.

Usually Uncle Charlie says *Drive safely, Ruby Nell,* but today he watches them leave without a word of caution. I've got to find out what's causing his unusual reserve with Mama.

But first, we have to save Lovie from the electric chair.

"Maybe we ought to get George up in his hot air balloon, Lovie." I think they fly those things after sunrise and before sunset, and the sun's just getting ready to vanish over Tupelo's western horizon.

"I think you should stay on the ground, dear hearts. Just talk to him casually and find out what you can." Uncle Charlie sits down beside me. "Before you go, there's something I have to tell you."

When he takes my hand, I get this sinking feeling that whatever he's fixing to say, it's not something I want to hear.

"Jack called. From Mexico."

This is *definitely* not something I want to hear. Though I never had cause to doubt his fidelity when we were officially married, we're not official anymore. With his killer looks and revved-up libido, he's bound to have landed in a passel of trouble. As much as I don't want to keep fighting him for custody of Elvis, I'm not fond of the idea that my almost-ex has run off with a doe-eyed senorita and will be sailing into the sunset in Cancún.

"He was in a little scrape," Uncle Charlie says.

"What kind of scrape?" I ask.

"He's been shot."

The world as I know it comes to an end. I am a widow and Elvis is fatherless.

"Quick, Lovie. Get her some water."

Lovie reaches into the cooler for a bottle of water and I drink till my head stops spinning and my chair settles back onto solid ground.

"Where? How?"

"He's going to be okay, Callie. The bullet didn't penetrate any major organs."

What was he doing to get shot? In Mexico, of all places? I don't know whether to get sick with worry or hop a plane and slap him silly.

"He'll be good as new in a few days. He said to tell you not to worry."

"If I'd wanted a life of worry I'd have married a Mafia hit man or a career criminal." For all I know, he could be both. "You tell Jack Jones . . ."

That I can't bear the thought of him bleeding? That when I thought he was dead I wanted to head to a cloister and take vows of eternal chastity?

I jump out of my chair but have to grab hold of the arms to stay upright.

Uncle Charlie steadies me. "Everything's going to be all right, dear heart."

I believe him, in spite of the fact that I'm currently more like the star of *The Trials and Tribulations of Pauline* than a grown woman having a real life. All I want is three children and a bulletproof husband. Is that asking too much?

"Can Elvis stay with you while we find George?"

Judging by my dog's droopy tail, I can tell he fancies himself going with me in the hot air balloon, maybe becoming one of those flying Elvises. Or Elvi, as I heard one misguided TV announcer say.

"I'll be glad to have the company. We'll be at Eternal Rest. I need to check on Bobby."

Bobby Huckabee from Pensacola, Uncle Charlie's new young (twenty-nine) assistant. What Bobby lacks in looks, he makes up for in dedication. Which is the reason Uncle Charlie could leave the funeral home long enough to oversee the festival.

Uncle Charlie's been trying to do everything by himself far too long. I'm not foolish enough to think he's planning retirement—he's much too vital for that—but it's high time for him to have some leisure for the things he loves. Like fishing.

"I don't know what time we'll be back," I tell Uncle Charlie, and he says, "Take your time. And be careful. If George acts the least bit suspicious, go to the police and let them handle it."

When I bend down to tell Elvis good-bye, he turns his back.

He loves the funeral home and considers himself its official ambassador. I don't know of another dog who gets to put on a bow tie and act as chief comforter to the bereaved. Still, you'd think I was consigning him to life with only bread and water.

With the final round of tribute artist competition over and blues great Big Bill Broonzy taking the stage, Lovie and I head into the crowd to search for our prime suspect.

"I don't know how we're going to get George to take us up in his balloon," I tell Lovie. "That's your department."

She says a word not meant for the fainthearted. Fortunately— or unfortunately, depending on how you look at it—my heart's having to grow more courageous every day.

"I'm not planning to jeopardize my relationship with Rocky over a man who can't keep his pecker in his pants. You're going to have to haul out your rusty flirting skills."

"They're not *that* rusty."

"Come on. There's George by the corn dog vendor. Prove it."

"You think I can't?"

Putting an extra swish in my hips, I head that way with Lovie goading me every step.

"You can do better than that. Come on, Callie. Shake that thing. Let's see the real stuff."

I know she means well. This is Lovie's way of cheering me on. Still, she's proving her point, too—that I've spent nearly a year pining over Jack, that I've lost interest in all things male since he

124

walked out the door and rode into the great beyond on his Harley Screamin' Eagle with the heated seats.

The thought of that hated Harley—not to mention Jack's latest scrape—transforms me into a woman no man is safe around. Believe me, I have no intention of letting somebody who gets shot in Mexico continue to tamper with my heart.

I swear, if you could harness my pheromones right now and convert them to solar power, you could light up New York.

George Blakely doesn't stand a chance.

Chapter 10

Sunsets, Pompadours, and Pig Pens

Before I know what hit me, I'm headed to George's hot air balloon. Suffice it to say, a woman fueled by indignation and scented with Jungle Gardenia is a lethal weapon.

The balloon is moored in the north section of the massive Bancorp South Convention Center's parking lot, walking distance from the festival if you don't mind crossing the railroad tracks on foot. Lovie, George, and I are game, though I'll have to say the heat takes its toll on him. Maybe Texas is not as humid as Mississippi or maybe George is not as physically fit as he looks. Or it could be that tight jumpsuit. Whatever the reason, by the time we get to the balloon, he's sweating like a mule on the back forty.

He takes a white handkerchief out of his pocket and mops his face before extending his hand to help us into the basket. It's roomier than I'd have imagined. And the view will be splendid. I can see over the sides, which appear to be tall enough for safety, especially as long as we're on the ground. I'll probably change my mind once we're airborne.

As we lift off the asphalt, we gather quite a crowd. The basket sways and so does my stomach.

I glance over to see how Lovie's faring, and she's hanging on for dear life. Strike hot air ballooning from our long list of things we want to do before we die.

Lovie and I have been keeping a list since we were eighteen. So far we've checked off some pretty dangerous pursuits. Spelunking and rock climbing top the list. Both Lovie's suggestions. Don't let her size fool you. She's the athletic, adventurous type. I'm more the quiet, artistic type. *Puccini opera in Florence* tops my list.

We're planning a trip to Italy next summer, unless she's so deeply involved with Rocky she can't bear to leave him. Then, of course, there's a small hitch with Elvis. If I were to leave him for three weeks, there's no telling what kind of revenge he'd take.

The balloon ascends in a slow, lazy kind of way. If I change my mind about this mode of transportation, there's still time to jump over the side without breaking major bones.

Naturally, I'd never leave Lovie, who is now flying high with her eyes closed.

"Isn't this great?" George says, and I nod my head, afraid if I open my mouth I'll lose lunch. He does something to the vales and other thinga-majiggies, and all of a sudden we swoosh upward so fast, bailing out is no longer an option. Skimming the tops of Jim's Barbecue and the Greyhound Bus Station, I risk a peek down.

My stomach lurches, then settles back into place. *I can do this.*

It's only when we waft over the top of the Tupelo Police Station that I realize I'm in the balloon with a possible killer and nowhere to run.

Whose bright idea was this, anyway? More to the point, what am I going to do if George confesses in midair?

I punch Lovie, who sneaks a peek, then shuts her eyes again. It's all up to me.

Turning my back to the view, I say, "So, George. There must be hundreds of tribute artist competitions. What brought you to Tupelo?"

He pulls out his handkerchief and mops his face again. If I didn't know he's a veteran ballooner, I'd say he didn't like swinging above the treetops in a puny basket any better than I do.

"It's the Birthplace." He gives me this funny look.

Okay, so I don't get any points for brilliant interrogation techniques. I'm new at this. It's not as if I plan to make criminal investigation my life's work.

"Is this your first time here?"

"No." Wincing, he grabs his stomach. "Barbecue."

"It'll get you if you're not used to it." *Strike that.* How could a Texan not be used to barbecue? "I guess you got to know our famous local impersonator well. Dick?"

George turns pale, twitches a time or two, then breaks out in a serious sweat. I never expected

128

such a reaction. I ram Lovie again in the ribs. *Hard.* If I'm going to face down a killer, I want a witness who's watching the action.

"Lovie has a theory about Dick's wife, Bertha."

"I do?"

I elbow her again to get her full attention. "Tell George what you were telling me." She can spin a lie that would fool a psychic. "Go on, Lovie. Don't be shy."

The balloon picks up speed at an alarming rate, and the Calvary Baptist Church steeple looms right in our path. *Holy cow.* Before Lovie can come up with a story, we're going to be skewered.

You'd think George would be altering our course. Instead he's starts jerking around like a man gone crazy.

Or having convulsions.

"Lovie. Quick," I yell, just as George topples over the side of the basket.

We lunge, the basket tilts, and we end up sprawled on George's bottom half while his top half dangles over Calvary Baptist. One false move and all three of us will spill out and spatter downtown Tupelo.

"Hold on tight, Lovie. Don't move."

"If I hold him any tighter, we'll be banned in Boston."

Trust Lovie.

"George, are you all right?" I guess he's too scared to answer. "I'm going to grab hold of you. Okay?"

Silence. I'm praying he's just fainted with all the excitement. Inching my hands upward, I latch on to his belt.

"Can you move your arms, Lovie?"

"What you want me to do? Pick his pocket?"

"Grab his belt. Now. On the count of three, pull. One, two, *pull*."

I haul backward as hard as I can, but George is still not moving. Come to think of it, neither is the basket.

"What's wrong?" Lovie says, and I ask, "Are you pulling?"

If the word she says filters through the church roof to the preacher's office, he'll have to call a special prayer meeting just for her.

"Let's try again, Lovie."

This time part of George inches into the basket, but it's only his pants. If we haul backward one more time, he's going to lose them.

"Hold it," I say. "Something's got George on the other end."

"Who do you think it is? St. Peter?"

If I knew a word, I'd say it. Fortunately I don't have language habits I'll have to clean up when I become a mother.

Lifting myself gingerly on one elbow, I crane my neck to see over George.

"It's the steeple, Lovie."

"He's hanging onto the steeple?"

"No. But his wig is."

The overblown, wiry pompadour I'd viewed as George's *unfortunate* hair now turns out to be his biggest fortune. If it weren't for that cheap mop of synthetic hair, he'd be on the pavement by now.

"Grab his legs, Lovie. We've got to pull him loose."

Easier said than done. A wad of wig as big as my fist is lodged on the steeple. We might as well be trying to separate George from a lock and chain.

The basket careens madly as we play tug-of-war with the steeple, but George doesn't budge. At the rate we're going we'll be suspended forever over Calvary Baptist Church. Country singers will write ballads about us and Lifetime TV will do a movie that will make fanatics revere our bones.

I'm too young for sainthood.

Lovie says, "What does he have this thing on with? Super-glue?"

"One more time, Lovie."

"I don't have one more pull in me."

"You're not a quitter. *Pull.*"

With Herculean effort that fractures ribs (I'm certain) we rip George's toupee loose from the steeple. All three of us topple backward and George lands at our feet.

Dead.

"See if he has a pulse, Lovie."

"Who do you think I am? Florence Nightingale?

131

If you want to check his pulse, be my guest." Lovie turns her back and retches over the side of the basket.

And that's when I notice we're no longer tethered to the church steeple; we're sailing east beheading trees and threatening planes. Even worse, nobody's steering. And sunset is approaching. *Balloon doom* time.

I leap into action. Actually what I do is stand in front of the mysterious mechanisms wondering how long we can stay aloft, whether the crash will kill us, and how long it will take somebody to discover three bodies in the basket.

Lovie staggers over looking like the victim of a train wreck and stands beside me, staring. I'd feel better if she'd try to do something, but still, it helps just having her close by.

Meanwhile, we're picking up speed. Soon we'll be out of Tupelo.

"We've got to do something," I tell Lovie, and she does.

She leans over the basket and yells, "Help." Before I snatch her bald-headed, I realize we're over the festival and maybe she's on to something, so I lean over the side and scream with her.

A few specks (translated: people so far away they can't possibly hear us) wave, and then we sail over the Birthplace and waft our merry way over East Tupelo's golf-ball-shaped water tower. Did I say *missing it by half an inch?*

Veering sharply, the balloon takes a southeasterly track. We're over farm county now, cotton and soybean fields, pastures and cows. We scare them so badly they'll never produce milk again.

Meanwhile the hiss and puff of the balloon hardware sounds repitilian. And I'm terrified of snakes.

Don't let anybody tell you balloon travel is romantic. Especially when there's another dead Elvis rolling around at your feet.

Lovie and I start twisting valves, knobs, and doodads while I invoke Mother Earth, Mother Teresa, and the *Spirit of St. Louis* (Charles Lindbergh's plane). For good measure, I send a plea toward Jude, the patron saint of lost causes.

When my cell phone rings, I nearly startle out of the basket. Scrambling on the floor of the basket while trying to avoid contact with the corpse, I dig it out of my purse.

The caller ID panel is lit with salvation.

"Uncle Charlie. Oh, thank goodness."

He was a pilot in Vietnam. Why didn't I think of him twenty minutes ago?

I babble out our latest predicament with Lovie making helpful comments on the side.

"Tell Daddy I don't want to be buried in pink. Tell him I don't want any preaching over my body. Tell him—"

"Shut up!" I yell, and she does, though I have every reason to believe I'll pay for this later.

"Stay calm, dear heart," Uncle Charlie says. "Tell me your location."

"What if I lose signal? What if we lose gas?"

Lovie says, "I don't think it's gas," and I give her a *look*.

"Callie, *Callie*." Uncle Charlie sounds rattled, a new twist for him. "Can you tell me where you are?"

"I don't know." From this vantage point, every farm looks alike. For all I know we could be in Alabama.

"What do you see?"

"Cows. A barn. A pigpen."

"Callie, listen to me. I want you to do everthing I tell you, okay?"

"Okay."

"I'm going to talk you down."

If I ever get my feet on terra firma again, I'm staying there.

Elvis' Opinion #6 on Mismatched Anatomy, Psychic Powers, and Guilt

Personally I never did believe George was guilty of anything except bad taste. Case in point, his wig.

Naturally I'm too polite to say *I told you so.* I just sit in the funeral home with my mismatched (but not so you'd notice) ears cocked and listen to both ends of Charlie's telephone conversation with Callie.

Some people think eavesdropping is tacky, but how else is a dog to figure out what his human mom needs? Forget all that mind-reading stuff. Dogs can read auras and smell spikes in temperature and divine the emotional terrain of their humans, but we're not psychic.

From the sound of things, it's going to take a whole lot of couch time to calm Callie down after this balloon escapade. (That would be me sitting on the sofa in her lap with no room left over for upstart cocker spaniels, thank you very much.)

While Charlie's talking Callie and Lovie out of the air, Bobby Huckabee comes into the office all primed to report on the embalming going on down in the basement.

How do I know this if I can't read minds? I happen to know the late great public school music teacher, Philestine Barber, is on the table, and I can smell Bobby's eagerness a mile.

Still on the phone, Charlie waves him to a seat, but Bobby squats down to scratch behind my ears. Charlie just hired him two weeks ago and we bonded instantly. Mostly because Bobby recognized my worth right off the bat, but also because he has mismatched eyes. One blue, the other green. You might say we formed a mismatched anatomy club.

Bobby claims his blue eye gives him psychic powers, and who am I to discourage him? Take every chance you get to feel good about yourself. That's my opinion.

Maybe we could crack this case if we'd enlist Bobby. I'll bet his visions would coincide exactly with my theories. Forget spurned lovers and card cheats. Whoever is knocking off these Elvises doesn't like their singing any better than I do.

Right now, though, my main concern is not who's guilty of murder; it's Callie.

Charlie's mopping his face while he talks with her. Listen, Charles Sebastian Valentine is one of the coolest men I know. He doesn't sweat; he just handles the problem. For him to show this kind of emotion, my human mom is in a heap of trouble.

If I were the worrying kind, I'd be gnawing my paws. But I'm not a worrywart; I'm a doer. I politely ease over to Charlie, get as close to the receiver as I can, and howl a few bars of "Amazing Grace."

I know my human mom better than anybody, *including* my human daddy, unfortunately. If he'd listened to me, he'd still be sitting pretty reading the Sunday morning paper in the gazebo, drinking fresh-squeezed orange juice, and enjoying Callie's big fat Stearns and Foster mattress. Among other things I'm not fixing to divulge outside this family.

But that's a whole 'nother consideration. Right now, the point is to get Callie down safely. She's a great believer in the power of prayer. Never mind that she's got this hodgepodge of angels and spirits and deities she turns to. The point is, her beliefs give her strength.

But nothing does it better than a great gospel song sung by the greatest singer of all time.

That would be yours truly, thank you very much.

"Is that Elvis?" I can hear the catch in her voice. "Oh, Uncle Charlie. Tell him I love him. Tell him I'll see him soon."

I never doubted it for a minute. Does a cat have a climbing gear? Then Charlie Valentine's going to get Lovie and my human mom down from that balloon.

Chapter 11

Pork Revenge, Hog Death, and Handcuffs

Hang on, Lovie!"

We grab the sides of the basket while the balloon plummets between a giant oak tree and a grape arbor. It rips off branches, collapses supports, and scatters grapes before it deposits us on the ground with teeth-jarring force. Lovie is thrown on top of dead Texas Elvis, but I manage to remain upright.

"Lovie, are you all right?"

"If you ever mention hot air balloon to me again, I'll shoot you."

I take that as a yes. Anxious to get out, I swing one leg over the side of the basket when I hear a roar of outrage. And it's not coming from my cousin.

Swiveling toward the left, I look right into the beady eyes of a mad boar hog. *Holy cow!* We've landed in the middle of the pigpen, and the head pig monster is bent on revenge.

I jerk my leg back so fast I topple into Lovie, who had barely gained her feet. While we huddle in a screaming heap, the rampaging hog rams the side of the basket with his snout.

My whole body is shaking and my head feels

funny, but I'm not about to be outdone by a farm animal.

"We've come too far for death by hog," I tell Lovie.

"What do you propose we do? Invite him to George's funeral?"

"Fight back."

"With what?" Lovie asks.

"Anything you can get your hands on." She reaches down and I add, "Except George."

"Spoilsport," she says, jerking off her boot (which she is fond of wearing with peasant skirts, even in summer).

I grab my purse and hit the hog over the head, yelling, "Shoo" while Lovie whacks him with her boot, a lethal weapon if I ever saw one. It's a size 8 with a steel-reinforced heel.

She whacks his snout and the mad hog retreats squealing his outrage.

"Lovie, *run*."

We hightail it over the basket toward the fence with me trying to keep up. Lovie scrambles over and I'm not far behind.

At last. Freedom.

Or not.

The lanky, sunbaked farmer who is suddenly standing over us in his dusty overalls doesn't look like the welcoming committee. More like a lynch mob.

"The grape arbor you gals took down with that contraption is going to cost you a pretty penny."

Furthermore, he's brought backup—the Lee County sheriff. Who doesn't look happy to see us, either.

"You again." Sheriff Trice gives Lovie the evil eye. At least that's what I'll call it when I retell this story. If I live to retell it. "What brings you to Plantersville in a balloon?"

Without waiting for an answer, he climbs over the fence and waves his hands at the mad hog, who trots off and starts rooting under an oak tree as if he never had any intention of ripping Lovie and me to shreds.

Any minute now Sheriff Trice is going to discover another dead Elvis.

I can't just sit here without reporting it first. That will make us look guilty. Getting up, I brush off the seat of my skirt, but after that race through the pigpen I don't even want to think about the state of my Burberry ballerinas.

"It was an unfortunate accident," I call after Sheriff Trice. "All of it."

Where's Lovie? Soon we're likely to be handcuffed and hauled off to jail, and she's over there under a sweet gum tree talking on her cell phone.

Sheriff Trice takes one look in the basket, uses his phone to call reinforcements, then strides back to me.

"You have some tall explaining to do."

"Well, Lovie and I were just—"

"Callie, stop." Thank goodness Lovie's back,

140

and judging by the fire and brimstone shooting from every pore, she's back in full force. "We're not saying another word. Daddy will be here in a minute with Grover Grimsley."

The family lawyer. Also my divorce attorney. Why didn't I think of that? With three dead impersonators, two of whom died practically in Lovie's arms, we're in trouble so deep neither my logic nor my cousin's charm is going to get us out of it.

Lovie and I stake out a spot under the sweet gum, and while we wait for Uncle Charlie and Grover, I have plenty of time to repent my hasty foray into murder detection. Why did I think I was capable of confronting a killer (who turned out to be another victim)? Why didn't I go home, pour myself a cup of green tea chai, sit on my front porch swing with Elvis at my feet, and wait for the law to handle things?

"How did you know where to tell Uncle Charlie to come?" I ask Lovie.

"While you were getting ready to spill your guts to Sheriff Trice, I asked that old coot his name." She nods in the direction of the farmer, who is now in the pigpen inspecting the balloon.

"Who is he?"

"Bruce Holland, one of the biggest farmers in Lee County."

Uncle Charlie arrives with Elvis and Grover in tow, and the sheriff proceeds to question us. It's mostly *who, what, when,* and *where?* I'll have to say I don't hear a thing that couldn't be answered without a lawyer present, but I'm not about to question Uncle Charlie's judgment. Who knows? If he hadn't brought Grover, I might be on my way to jail now instead of heading back to Tupelo to collect my alter ego (translated: my Dodge Kick-Ass Ram).

Listen, if you'd come as close to death as I have today, you'd allow yourself a little *word*. Maybe two. After all, I'm only *thinking* it.

When we arrive at our parked vehicles, Uncle Charlie says, "This case is getting too dangerous. I believe it's best if we let the law handle it. Both of you go home and get some rest."

"What about Philestine Barber?" I ask.

She was one of my regulars. I was planning to do her makeup tonight and fix her trademark hairdo, the French twist. I'm so good at making the dearly departed look natural, my regulars make post-mortem beauty appointments before they even get sick.

"It can wait till morning," Uncle Charlie says, and I'm not about to argue. I'm too relieved to have the rest of the evening for myself.

So is Lovie. She heads home saying she's going to soothe herself with chocolate while I strike out to Mooreville with nothing in mind except a hot bath.

The first thing I do when I get home is feed Hoyt and Elvis plus seven stray cats. I've been meaning to find good homes for the cats, but they've been here nearly a year and so far I haven't even looked. Pretty soon they'll have squatters' rights. Maybe I should just go ahead and name them.

Hoyt and the cats get regular fare, but I put Fit 'N Trim in Elvis' bowl. The battle of Elvis' bulge is a losing proposition. No matter what I feed him, Mama and Lovie sabotage his diet with forbidden treats.

After the pets are fed I climb into the shower and scrub myself clean, then emerge feeling almost human again. Even though it's not even close to bedtime, I put on clothes that make me feel as if somebody (Jack, if you want to know the truth) has wrapped his arms around me and said *it's okay, you can rest now.* Pajamas and my blue summer robe. Then I tie my hair with a blue ribbon and slide my feet into blue satin mules with ostrich plumes on the toe. The death of another impersonator is no reason to let fashion and beauty slip.

Next I make a steaming cup of green tea chai (my comfort drink of choice), then switch on the TV and curl onto the sofa with Elvis. I can tell he's feeling the sting of rejection after being gone from me all afternoon.

Hoyt rounds the corner looking cute and comical. I try to get him on the sofa with me, but there doesn't seem to be any room, so he just curls on top of my feet.

I try to get involved in the TV show, a funny

143

rerun of *I Love Lucy*, which I deliberately chose because I don't want to watch anything that smacks of blood and guts.

But something keeps niggling at my mind. Finally it hits me: the diary.

I hate unfinished business. Hurrying upstairs, I retrieve Bertha's forgotten journal from my night-stand. When I come back down, Elvis is hogging the couch so Hoyt can't jump up. My basset looks so disgruntled I laugh.

What would I do without my pets? With the love and loyalty of good animals, you can get through anything, including having your almost-ex leave you on a major family holiday and then go off and get shot in Mexico. And that's not counting all the loneliness in between.

Jack had no business going off down there doing no telling what in the first place. No wonder he never wanted children. He was too busy running all over the country like a wildman.

I'm not even going to think about who shot him or why. Or where, for that matter.

And I especially won't think about why I still harbor tenderness for a man like that.

Instead I nestle into the sofa again with Elvis and start reading Bertha's diary. She writes about Dick's numerous affairs in great detail, but it's hard to tell truth from fiction. I know she lied in her diary about Lovie. How many other women were Dick's lovers only in Bertha's imagination?

Bertha is no Jane Austen, so most of what she writes almost puts me to sleep. And with small wonder. After the day I've had it's a miracle I'm upright.

Yawning, I get up to make another cup of chai. So far I've learned nothing that will shed light on the recent murders. All I know for certain is that George's death blows my theory that he was the killer.

I'm heading back to my sofa when the phone rings. Gas, Grits, and Guts pops up on the caller ID. *Good grief.* Is it Fayrene calling to say something has happened to Mama?

I snatch up the receiver and say a breathless "hello."

"Callie?" It's Jarvetis. "Fayrene told me not to call you, but if I was in your shoes I'd want to know."

I'm going to have a heart attack. "Know what?"

"Ruby Nell took a little spell over in Tunica and they're staying overnight."

"Is Mama in the hospital?"

"No. Fay said it was just a sinking spell and Ruby Nell didn't feel like driving. I thought you ought to know."

"Thanks, Jarvetis."

Mama has her secrets, but it's not like her to withhold health information. For one thing, she's a drama queen and loves the attention she gets when she's sick.

I dial her cell phone. "Mama?" She sounds

145

mighty perky for somebody at death's door. "Are you sick?"

"No. Why?"

"Jarvetis called and said you were."

"Oh, that."

"What does *oh, that* mean, Mama?" I hear the distinct tinkle of coins pouring out of a slot machine. "Are you in the casino?"

"You knew Fayrene and I were going to do a little recreational gambling after the senior citizens' dance. Something came up and we decided to overnight it."

"What things? And why did Jarvetis say you were sick?"

"Well, if you must know, Fayrene told Jarvetis that to get him off our backs. The old coot. All he wants to do is pump gas, raise bird dogs, and draw Social Security. Fayrene tried to get him to take dancing, but *no*, he had to be a stick in the mud. Live a little, that's what I told Fayrene."

"Mama, you shouldn't be in the middle of their marital rifts, and you certainly shouldn't lie to Jarvetis. Poor man."

I'd hate to have Mama and Fayrene ganged up against me.

"*I* didn't lie."

"But you're a party to it."

"What are you now? A lawyer? Loosen up, Carolina. Maybe if you'd lighten up a bit, Jack would come home where he belongs."

146

"Sidetracking me won't work, Mama. What is this *thing* that came up?"

"That's for me to know and you to find out."

She hangs up. I've a good mind to call her back and beg her to be sensible, but all in all I'd rather have a mother who's having a bit too much fun than one who's sitting home feeling sorry for herself and whining because I'm not at her beck and call. Thank goodness, Mama's not that type.

Going back into the living room, I resume reading. I'm well into my second cup of chai when Bertha leaves Dick's affairs behind and starts writing about her own. My drink forgotten, I read as fast as I can.

Holy cow. If Bertha's telling the truth, I might have just solved this case.

This is momumental. And much too important for a mere phone call. I change into jeans and a pair of cute Ferragamo sandals with turquoise beads, tuck my dogs into bed, tell them to use the doggie door if they need to potty, then climb into my Dodge and head back to Tupelo.

Chapter 12

Costumes, Boyfriends, and Unexpected Developments

Painted pink with a wooden shingled roof and stained glass windows, Lovie's house looks like a fairy-tale cottage. You expect to see unicorns lounging under the magnolia trees and a Cheshire cat or two lurking in the branches.

Considering her enchanted house and her penchant for shocking, I'm not surprised when she comes to the front door wearing a majorette costume complete with tasseled boots.

"Are you having a costume party, Lovie?"

"A party for one." Instead of leading me inside and plying me with chocolate confections (her mission in life is to fatten me up), she eases the front door shut. That leaves us standing under her front porch light in plain view of any neighbor or passerby who cares to look this way. "Rocky's inside."

Meaning she has plans for him that are strictly private. I get the picture. Believe me, I don't want to interfere, but I don't want to drop the ball on murder, either.

"I didn't know you expected him so soon, Lovie."

"He wanted to surprise me. I picked him up at the airport about an hour ago."

"I should have called first, but I was too excited."

"What gives?"

"Bertha's diary." A car cruises past her house and I get the creepy feeling the driver is watching. Female. Is it Bertha? "We need to talk, but not out here."

"Come in. Rocky knows all about the murders. Maybe he can help."

Though he has been back to Tupelo a few times, I haven't seen Rocky since the Bubbles Caper. But I don't blame Lovie for keeping him under wraps in the early throes of courtship. Everybody in northeast Mississippi would have an opinion, especially the Valentine family. Including yours truly. Nothing tears up a relationship faster than listening to the bad advice of friends and family.

We get inside and Rocky is sitting on the sofa in a suit and tie with his brown hair carefully combed. He'd look like an oversized preacher making a Sunday afternoon call if it weren't for his cowlick and his amazing golden laserlike eyes. Rocky Malone is an intriguing combination of teddy bear, little boy, and man of mystery who might not do to mess with. No wonder Lovie's over the moon.

She offers coffee and brownies, but I tell her I won't be staying that long. If there's the least chance Lovie can find happiness with this man, I intend to do everything in my power to make it happen.

When she sits down, he reaches for her hand

and gazes at her like she's a star that just fell out of a southern summer sky. This is the stuff of every woman's dreams and I find myself fighting a burst of envy.

It's not that I begrudge her this romantic interlude. But sometimes, when I see another couple holding hands or sharing a quick kiss in the Barnes Crossing Mall parking lot, I want to race home and join Match.com. Or move somewhere so Jack doesn't waylay me around every corner. In my most desperate moments I even think about going to one of those church socials for singles where the only available men wear their belts under their armpits and comb one long twig of hair across their bald spots.

Right now, though, I have to pack up my hopes and get through the evening.

Lovie's as close as she can get without being in Rocky's lap, and the way she's caressing his leg with the toe of her majorette boot, I can tell she wants more from him than being put on a pedestal. But he just smiles and pats her hand.

Obviously these two have vastly different ideas about courtship. I'd better get out of here fast so they can work out their differences.

I make quick work of small talk with Rocky—*did you have a good trip? We're glad to have you*—that sort of thing. Then I get right to the reason I shucked comfortable pajamas and hurtled into the city.

"Bertha's diary chronicles her affairs in great detail. There's no doubt she was cozy with George Blakely. *And* Brian Watson."

"Two of the dead Elvis impersonators," Lovie explains to Rocky. "The other victim was her husband."

"Is she like the black widow spider?" he asks. "First sex, then murder?"

"Bingo," I say. "My theory, exactly."

"Are you turning the diary over to the police?" is his next question.

Lovie and I exchange a look. *No way.* Not with its damning implications against her.

"Not yet," I tell him. "There's more. Bertha's also having an affair with Thaxton Miller. If nothing has changed since the last entry, she's still seeing him."

"Do you think she plans to kill Thaxton, too?" Lovie asks.

Ordinarily she'd have said a word, but it looks like she has moderated her language in honor of her new boyfriend, which raises him another notch on my suitability radar.

"It's enough of a possibility that I don't want you in the middle of this, sweetheart," Rocky tells Lovie.

Well, glory hallelujah. Has my cousin finally found her prince?

Rocky puts his arm around her, and I'll have to say if you needed somewhere to hide, behind him

151

would be a good idea. Not only is he the size of a Whirlpool side-by-side refrigerator, but he also has the look of somebody whose body is bullet-proof—lots of muscle and very little fat.

"You should be careful, too, Callie," he says.

I like it that he's concerned about Lovie's family. Wouldn't it be great if Rocky could fill the role of the older brother I always wanted but never had?

"You're right," I tell him. "We need to proceed with caution. Lovie, there's no need for you to come to the festival tomorrow."

Leaving Lovie to lie low and the two of them to work out their courtship differences, I drive home with an eye peeled toward the dark. Who knows what lurks out there?

That's what happens when your courtyard is surrounded by crime tape, your cousin is suspected of murder, and your ex-protector is shot in Mexico. You get paranoid.

To take my mind off death I turn on the radio, but wouldn't you know? In honor of the festival, the local DJs are playing Elvis. "Jailhouse Rock." Which only makes me worry about Lovie being locked up behind bars.

The diary is not enough hard evidence to turn the police's attention from Lovie to Bertha. I'm not fixing to let them get their hands on it. Their focus is still the means, and it was Lovie, not Bertha, who prepared food for the festival as well as my ill-fated party.

As soon as the autopsy reveals the type of poison, I'll look into that myself. Meanwhile, I climb into bed trying to figure out how I'm going to stop Bertha from killing Love Me Tender Elvis and nail her for offing three other impersonators.

The first thing I do when I wake up is call Mama to see if she and Fayrene are back from their little overnighter. She doesn't answer her cell or her home phone, which—knowing Mama—strikes terror in my heart. But instead of visions of her lying in a hospital somewhere with a heart attack, I picture her so tired after an all-night stint of gambling and partying that even an earthquake couldn't wake her.

I hope she's only been partying with Fayrene, but considering the *something else* that came up and her recent display in my courtyard with Texas Elvis—God rest his soul—there's no telling what Mama's up to.

I call Uncle Charlie to relate what I learned from Bertha's diary and see what he thinks about tailing her before she can kill again.

"Let's let the law handle it, Callie. With a killer on the loose and the festival still going strong, things are getting too dangerous for you and Lovie to be in the middle of it."

He has a good point. I'll be only too glad to get back to my normal life where nothing more exciting happens than Elvis stealing Hoyt's bone and Trixie Moffett getting miffed because I cut her hair a quarter inch shorter than she wanted, never mind that the cut is more flattering to her little fox face and besides that, is the latest New York style.

I consider asking if Uncle Charlie has heard any news from Jack, but I'm trying to wean myself from worrying over my almost-ex. He's on his own now. He'll just have to muddle through without me.

Worry is no excuse for letting my exercise habit slip. This is one of the areas where Jack and I parted company. He's a spur-of-the-moment man, given to abrupt comings and goings without forethought and planning. And certainly without revealing those plans to me.

While I'm flexible when the need arises, I'm mostly the kind of woman who thrives on routine.

Not wanting to interrupt anything, I don't call Lovie, either. Though I'm dying to know how she fared with Rocky last night.

After a breakfast of oatmeal with strawberries, I change into loose jogging pants and Nike Airs. I also strap on my gun. A killer's out there somewhere and I don't intend be a statistic before I have a chance to be a mother.

I just hope I don't have to use it. I'm no firearms expert, but in a pinch I *can* hit a target . . . if it stands still long enough.

Though my backyard is big enough for Elvis to

get his share of romping, he needs to work off some girth, so I grab his leash.

Elvis and I head down the street past Leonora Moffett's, whose little shih tzu spies us from the screened-in front porch and barks his head off. Sometimes Elvis barks back just to show him who's in charge of the neighborhood, but today he royally ignores the shih tzu.

I have to keep track of my walks by time, not blocks. Unincorporated and not likely to get that way in the next hundred years, Mooreville doesn't have blocks. It has streets, a few paved, most not, with glamorous names such as County Road 1820. Fayrene has up a petition to name our street Honeysuckle Lane, which makes sense considering the proliferation of the heavily scented southern vine.

Some people think the first sign of spring is daffodils, but in this neck of the woods it's the sound of weed eaters doing battle with honeysuckle. It tries to take over mailboxes, fence posts, dog houses, and everything else that's standing still and hasn't already fallen victim to kudzu.

So far the county supervisors (our governing entity) have managed to shuffle her proposal to the bottom of the pile.

At the end of the street where Fayrene and Jarvetis live, we turn into the cul-de-sac. TV 9's popular weatherman Butch Jenkins (famous because at the first hint Mississppi might get a flake of snow, he does a snow dance) is in his front yard spraying roses. From the looks of things, he might as well have saved his energy. Black spot blight and aphids have already beat him to the punch.

Usually I'd stop to chat—mostly about gardening, which I adore—but today I don't have time for socializing. I just wave and keep on trotting.

Rounding the end of the cul-de-sac, I head back, but Elvis has other ideas. Lifting his leg on mailbox posts, for one. Nosing around other people's yards, for another.

"Come on, boy. Let's get home."

No matter how I coax and tug, he refuses to budge. Sometimes I think he does this deliberately to show me who's boss.

"All right, you win. Pup-Peroni treats."

He comes running, which is not saying much. With his short basset legs and his portly figure, the most he can do is lumber along with his ears flopping.

Suddenly he skids to a halt. Now what?

"Elvis. *Come.*"

He gives me this *look,* which I'll swear he's been practicing with Mama, then heads my way.

Limping. And *bleeding. Holy cow!*

He could bleed to death before I get him to Dr. Sandusky's clinic in Tupelo. Whipping out my cell phone, I call Lovie.

"Quick. Give me directions to that veterinary clinic in Mantachie." Run by Luke Champion, if memory serves.

Mantachie is only ten minutes from home. Lovie carried Elvis a few weeks ago as a favor to me.

I scoop up Elvis and run while I listen to Lovie. If he's badly hurt, I'll never get over it. I'll have to hit every shoe sale in Tupelo just to make myself get out of bed in the morning.

"Do you need me, Callie? I can meet you at the clinic."

"Thanks, Lovie. I think I've got it covered."

When I ease my dog into the passenger side of my Dodge Ram, he whimpers. *Poor Elvis.*

"Don't worry, boy. We're going to get help."

Just out of the driveway I remember poor old Philestine Barber waiting for my magic touch at the funeral home. After I maneuver onto the highway I grab my cell phone to tell Uncle Charlie I've been delayed.

Thank goodness the Elvis competition is over (though not the festival), and I won't be needed downtown to fix pompadours.

"Don't worry, dear heart. Philestine's viewing is not until three this afternoon. Is Ruby Nell back?"

This sounds like a throwaway question, but when Uncle Charlie speaks, you'd better pay attention because everything he says has purpose.

"She's not back yet. But I'm sure she'll be home in time for the funeral."

Mama provides the music at Eternal Rest. Even she wouldn't go so far as to have *other things* going on when Uncle Charlie needs her.

Strangely, he doesn't respond to this news of Mama.

"Take care of Elvis. And remember . . . 'Hope is the thing with feathers that perches in the soul and sings the tune without words and never stops at all.'"

In times of deepest distress, Uncle Charlie loves to quote the great poets and writers. Usually it's Shakespeare, but today it's Emily Dickinson. I don't know why, but his little quotations always make me feel better.

Elvis' Opinion #7 on Vets, Cats, and Fate

First of all, let me set the record straight: I did *not* step on that piece of broken glass to garner sympathy. I don't like pain.

Furthermore, if I wanted Callie's sympathy I'd think of a much better way to get it. Take last night, for instance. All I had to do was bat my basset eyes and droop my tail a little, and she had me on the couch before you could howl the first bar of "Love Me."

As for showing her who's boss, I try to keep that low-key— like looking cute when she gets herself a snack so she'll give me a treat, even though she's put me on a diet that wouldn't sustain one of her dratted, aggravating stray cats. Or showing my teeth to Hoyt when she's not looking so he won't horn in on my territory. Callie's lap is my private domain, thank you very much, and I'll thank him to keep his dirty paws off.

She's whizzing north on Highway 371 exceeding the speed limit, which is not like her. I ease over and put my head in her lap so she'll slow down, so she'll see that I'm not fixing to haul off and die.

Listen, I'm a young buck. I still have lots of living and loving to do. Not to mention that I have lots left to teach my human mom.

How to hold on to hope, for one thing. Lately she's been discouraged about the stalemate between her and my human daddy. I want to teach her to pay attention to every single detail of her life every day, not just when things are going great, but on those days when she feels hopeless and lonely, when she believes she's destined to a future empty of children and the love of a good man.

Revel in the simple joys, I say. Give thanks for slow lazy mornings when you can loll on the front porch in the sunshine and let a breeze blow your ears back. Get excited about rolling in the grass and listening to Jack coax the blues out of his harmonica. Be grateful you can still eat fried chicken and not fart.

Callie's foot eases off the gas pedal, and I lift my head to watch the scenery. Nothing much is stirring this early in the morning except a few Holstein cows. This is farm county, the kind that makes a dog want to get out and find a cow patty or two to roll in. I've done it a few times on Ruby Nell's farm, but it puts Callie in such a state I've decided to forgo bovine cologne in favor of more socially acceptable fragrances. Dirt, for instance. There's nothing quite as relaxing as tumbling around in a good dusty hole, and Callie's okay with that.

The clinic rolls into view and she has me out of the truck so fast I don't have time to get irritated over the cats pictured on Luke Champion's wooden shingle out front, let alone heist my leg on his petunias.

There's a cute young chick at the reception desk who looks about the age of my bobby-socks fans (though they're likely in wheelchairs by now). She's probably some kid doing summer work till school starts. Chickie baby takes one look at Callie's stricken face and the blood all over her shirt, then goes running toward the back yelling, "Doc!"

See, I told you she was just a kid.

Luke Champion hustles out, all business till he sees my human mom. You could strike a match on the sparks.

"Let's see what we have here." He whisks me toward the back room with Callie trailing along beside us asking, "Is he going to be all right?"

The table's cold and hard as brickbat (vet's examining tables always are), but I'm don't complain. Listen, anybody who can survive being mauled by thousands of screaming fans can endure a bit of discomfort in a town hardly bigger than one of my signature Cadillacs.

Still, you'd think they'd put a blanket or something on the table when they see me coming. It's not every clinic in northeast Mississippi that gets graced with the dog who changed the face of music.

"The wound is not deep," the vet says. "I'll clean

it out, put in a couple of stitches, and he'll be good as new."

"I can't tell you how relieved I am. Thank you, Dr. Champion."

"My friends call me Champ."

This man works fast, and I'm not just talking about his medical skills. While he's swabbing and stitching, he's eyeing Callie like a Thoroughbred stallion checking out a filly he's planning to breed. And bless'a my soul, she's looking right back.

Listen, things in this life don't happen by chance. Any fool can look at the changing of seasons, the choreography of stars and planets, the movement of tides, and know Somebody Up There is in charge.

For instance, take me meeting my cute little Frenchie. If I hadn't escaped that day and if Ann-Margret hadn't been at Gas, Grits, and Guts, we might never have had our romantic rendezvous behind Mooreville Truck Stop.

It looks like fate has just given a great big nod to my human mom and my new vet.

I know she loves Jack, but what red-blooded woman who thinks she's been ditched for a moto-cycle wouldn't perk up under the admiring scrutiny of a handsome blue-eyed man? Besides being vulnerable, Callie's biological clock is ticking and she's just stumbled onto prize-winning daddy stock.

If Jack knows what's good for him, he'll get his shot-up butt on a plane and hightail it back to Mooreville. And if he doesn't start taking my love advice, he's likely to find himself outside Callie's fence looking in.

Which reminds me, I'm going to find myself in the same predicament if I don't dig a hole to freedom and mosey on down to check on Ann-Margret. Just because a French poodle's not in heat doesn't mean she wants to be ignored by her personal hunk 'a burning love.

After my paw is all bandaged up, Doc gives me two doggie bones, further proof he's trying to get on Callie's good side. When he sets me back on the floor, a sneaky Siamese minces around the corner and gives me the evil eye, then switches her tail like she's queen of the walk.

Doc calls her *Puss* and Callie calls her *precious*. I'd call her *history* if Doc hadn't filled me so full of medicine I'm seeing double and walking wobbly.

One thing I can't abide is an uppity cat.

I'm about to call for a wheelchair and get the heck out of Mantachie when Doc scoops me up and escorts Callie back to her pickup.

If he wants to be my personal slave, that's all right with me, Mama.

"Nice chassis." He puts his hand on the hood, but take it from me, he's not talking about her truck.

As we head back down the road, Callie looks over at me and says, "Champ's a really nice man. Don't you think so?"

How can I not agree? Doc has gentle hands and a kindly manner. In addition, he understands that if he wants to get on Callie's good side, he's got to bribe the boss. That would be yours truly.

I thump my tail but get distracted when I spot a hawk circling over the oak trees on our right. If I could sneak off down here, maybe get my old pal Trey (Jarvetis' best redbone hound) to go with me, we'd have a high old time. That hound's got a nose like Jimmy Durante; he can smell a fat rabbit a mile. I howl a bit of "Ain't Nothin' but a Hound Dog" just on general principles.

"After all, I'm not *really* married," Callie says. "Of course, *legally* I'm still Jack's wife. But we've been separated a year. Well, almost."

I can tell she wants me to agree, but much as I like pleasing my human mom, I'm not about to be a party to a love triangle that involves my human dad.

Though, come to think of it, having another man in the picture might not be such a bad idea. Maybe if Jack sees another man going after the woman he still considers his, he'll come to his senses and start revving up the charm he used to win her in the first place.

Belatedly I thump my tail again and inch over to lick her hand so she understands that if she wants the vet's slippers under her bed, I won't pee on them.

"I *knew* you'd agree with me. Not that I'm planning on doing anything with Champ. For goodness' sake, he hasn't even asked me out. But it never hurts to plan ahead."

Happy now, Callie whips out her cell phone to tell Charlie we're on the way to Eternal Rest after she takes care of her eleven o'clock beauty shop regular. I'm always happy to go to the funeral home. Not only does Charles Sebastian Valentine understand my finer qualities, but he's a straight-up man.

Callie wheels by the house to ditch the blood-stained clothes, but I notice she doesn't ditch the gun. Thanks to my tutorial skills, she's beginning to learn that she's a precious person worth spilling a little blood and guts over.

Jack gave her the weapon, and she hated the target practice he insisted on, but since then she's been down to the farm more than once to sharpen her skills.

The beauty shop regular is Roy Jessup, owner of Mooreville Feed and Seed, who's not ashamed to let it be known he prefers a sophisticated cut at Hair.Net to the skinned-neck look he'd get at a barbershop. Just between you and me, I think he comes here mostly to pick information out of Callie about his girlfriend, Trixie Moffett. Like her cousin Leonora, she's not the "Stand by Your

Man" type. (Now, *there* was a big talent, that Tammie Wynette. She put Tremont on the map. Of course, it was nothing like what I did for Tupelo and Memphis.)

After we finish at Hair.Net, we head to the funeral home, where Charlie carries me downstairs so we can keep Callie company while she pretties up Philistine for her journey into Glory Land.

Charlie puts me in his lap and scratches my ears while he reads *The Dream* by Edna St. Vincent Millay. He believes he's merely entertaining us with good poetry, but I see the heartbreak behind the words, hear his longing for Minrose and the long, sweet summer days when the fish were jumping, his blood was singing, and his true love was only a heartbeat away.

All the more reason he should forget about trying to keep Ruby Nell out of trouble and find a good woman of his own.

Maybe I'll sniff out one for him. After all, I'm a stellar judge of character and the best sleuth in the family.

Chapter 13

Guns, Perps, and Poison

Thank goodness nobody has noticed the gun strapped to my leg, not even the incredibly appealing Luke Champion.

I'm glad Uncle Charlie's was occupied with poetry because I never expected to have a new man on my mind, and I need some time to ponder. While I'm applying pancake to Philistine's remains, I picture Champ's hands on Elvis.

My philosophy is that you can tell a lot about a man from his hands. Champ's were suntanned and strong, but at the same time gentle. (I *love* his nickname. Reminds me of heroes.)

Unlike Lovie, who enjoys speculating about how a man's hand will feel on her erogenous zones (according to her, *all* her zones are erogenous), I like to imagine how a man's hands will look cradling a baby, pushing a carriage, changing a diaper, giving a 3:00 a.m. bottle.

"Well, looks like you and Elvis got into trouble while I was gone."

Mama sashays through the door wearing one of her notorious caftans designed to make her look like the queen of a small island. Bound for her to throw us off the scent of her own escapades by making a big todo over Elvis' bandaged paw.

Uncle Charlie doesn't ask about the dance or even why she stayed out overnight. Another twist in their newly cool relationship.

He says hello without adding *dear heart,* and she flounces into a chair without saying a word to him. I've got to get to the bottom of this.

"I guess Philistine's funeral's tomorrow." Mama's looking at a wall sconce and might as well be addressing Elvis.

"Two p.m.," Uncle Charlie says.

"I guess you want me to do the music."

"It's up to you."

"Since when has anybody else played the organ at Eternal Rest? It would be sacrilege." Mama pulls out a cigarette and crams it into a holder that would have been right at home with Greta Garbo, then deliberately starts smoking just to get our goats. She *never* smokes unless she's upset or mad at us.

There goes a quiet time of poetry and peace down the drain. To make matters worse, some woman has sneaked in upstairs and started pitching a hissy fit. Since the only corpse we currently have is Philistine, it has to be somebody looking to bury the newly deceased.

Uncle Charlie seems disinclined to get out of his chair (brand-new behavior for him) so I ask, "Where's Bobby Huckabee?"

"Running errands. Can you see who that is, dear heart?"

I'm finished with Philistine, anyway. It won't hurt me to handle business upstairs while Uncle Charlie and Mama work out whatever's eating them.

You'll never guess who's storming around the foyer acting like she's grieving over a beloved but very dead Dick. *Bertha*. Sporting widow's weeds—a black skirt and black buttoned-up jacket. Also a bad haircut glued to her skull with so much cheap hairspray I feel like I'm running along behind a mosquito truck.

"I thought I was going to have to call out the National Guard to get some attention around here."

Bertha pulls a handkerchief out of a purse as big as Pennsylvania and starts squalling her crocodile tears. Considering that she's been sleeping with every man who owns a sequined jumpsuit and probably knocked off her husband, to boot, I don't jump to comfort her.

As a mater of fact, I may have to shoot her. I'm glad I've got my gun.

"May I help you?"

"My husband's body has finally been released."

Which means the forensic specialists have found what they need for toxicology reports. Not that I'm getting involved; I'm taking Uncle Charlie's advice and getting back to normal. Still, it won't hurt to find out what she knows.

"I want to pick out caskets," she says. "Something cheap."

Bertha snorts into her handkerchief again. Probably to cover her last remark. Well, naturally she wouldn't want to spend much money on a man she's been cheating on right and left.

"We don't carry *cheap,* but we do have a line that's very affordable. This way please."

As I lead her toward the casket room I figure now is the best opportunity I'll get to dig for information. Forget that she got my hackles up and I'd as soon coat her with peanut butter and hang her out for the birds as look at her. I can turn on the charm when I put my mind to it.

Normally I'm not a mean and spiteful person, but anybody who claims she needs the National Guard to get the attention of the best funeral director in Mississippi has a long way to go before she can get back on my good side.

"It must be a relief to finally know what killed your husband," I tell her. "Did they identify the poison?"

"What does it matter? He's dead, one way or the other."

"I'm so sorry." I lead her to a simple gray casket without ornamentation. "This is our most popular economy brand."

"It'll do."

"Fine. I'll get papers so you can fill out the obituary information."

"Later. I have things to do."

Like killing Thaxton Miller?

I race downstairs to tell Uncle Charlie that Dick's body will be arriving, but the widow didn't stay long enough to complete funeral arrangements. The atmosphere is icy down here, and it's certainly not due to the air-conditioning.

"Mama, are you going back to Everlasting Monuments?"

"Naturally. I have a business to run."

She stands up and sprays herself with a flacon of Michael from her straw purse, a ploy deliberately calculated to make us wonder what she's up to now. The only good thing I can say about Mama's perfume is that she still wears a fragrance named after my daddy. (Technically speaking it's named for designer Michael Kors, but don't try to tell anybody in our family it's not named for Michael Valentine.)

"At least Philistine had the good sense to be creative when she preordered her tombstone."

"What did she want on it, Mama?"

" 'Gone to sing solo in the heavenly choir.' Now, that's my kind of woman."

Mama marches out and I have to run along behind to see if she will take Elvis back to Mooreville. His medicine has kicked in and he'll probably sleep the rest of the day. Maybe even into the night.

"Of course I will," she says.

"Take him straight to my house, Mama. I want him to be comfortable in his own bed."

"What are you going to be doing?"

"Festival."

Bertha didn't *say* she was going there, but it makes sense if she's planning to snuff out another Elvis.

Thank goodness Mama doesn't sniff out my little white lie. What I'm going to be doing is tailing Bertha, the exact opposite of Uncle Charlie's advice. He's nearly always right and I nearly always go along, but how can I sit back and let Bertha poison another Elvis impersonator? That's just un-American.

While Mama goes back to get Elvis, I whip out my cell phone and race toward my Dodge Ram.

"Lovie, what are you doing?"

"Having a Calgon Take Me Away moment."

"In the middle of the day?"

"Rocky's coming over and I'm planning a sneak attack."

"Meaning you're going to pretend you lost track of time and greet him at the door wearing nothing but bubbles."

"Among other things." I don't even want to know. "You sound distressed, Callie. What's up?"

"Nothing I can't handle." *I hope.* "Have fun, Lovie."

I peel out of the parking lot hoping I can find Bertha in the festival crowd and that I'm not too late to save Thaxton.

172

• • •

It's funny, when there's not a single living soul in your house except you and the pets, all you can see is couples. Running around the festival searching for Bertha I spot middle-aged married couples with their arms around each other, teenaged kids with body piercings and tattoos lip-locked in the middle of Main Street, geriatrics holding hands, even stray dogs rendezvousing in the alleys.

The sight makes me want to run home, lock the front door, and inspect myself for fatal flaws. I know, *I know.* Jack's leaving was not my fault. (Not entirely his, either. I pride myself on being nonjudgmental.) Still, no matter what or who causes a breakup, the pain is just as intense. I've heard women who wanted a divorce so badly they'd have killed for it to say they cried themselves to sleep every night for six weeks after they actually signed the papers.

I guess this angst has to do with loss and knowing that every little thing is left up to you. Even the hard stuff like getting stuck in a hot air balloon with a murder victim and not having anybody to run home and tell it to—the equivalent of paying a gazillion bucks an hour to lie on a psychiatrist's couch and relieve yourself of every messy ounce of guilt, shame, and fear.

My stomach growls, reminding me that I haven't had lunch, and no wonder I'm running around here conjuring up a pity party all over a public place. I hustle over to the refreshment booth, where Beulah Jane and Tewanda descend on me like a pair of Walt Disney fairy godmothers.

Beulah Jane leads me inside the booth to a chair while Tewanda waves an Elvis fan in front of my face.

"You look like you've seen a ghost," Tewanda says, and Beulah Jane, not to be outdone, says, "It's the heat, Tewanda. Pour her some iced peach tea to cool her off."

"Thanks, I'll take some of Lovie's barbecued ribs, too."

She made enough to sustain Hannibal's army on their march over the Alps. And they are particularly delicious, not the Memphis Rendezvous' dry ribs so many people rave about, but good old southern wet barbecue, lots of ketchup and vinegar and honey with just a hint of pineapple.

When I'm feeling more like a human being, I tell them about Dick's body being released.

"We heard." Tewanda takes my empty plate and dumps it in the garbage can, then sits down beside me and starts to fan herself. "I don't believe it was arsenic or strychnine, though. Do you remember what they called it, Beulah Jane?"

"Exotic, is all they said. I think they're still trying to identify it."

These two geriatrics are discussing poison the way you'd talk about whether to have sugar or lemon with your tea. Maybe that's what comes with age, a calm acceptance of life's ever-changing stage play, comic one minute, tragic the next, and always, always on-the-edge-of-your-seat suspenseful.

Or else Twenada and Beulah Jane don't want to get excited and get their blood pressures up.

"Did they find anything in the food or drink samples?" I ask.

"Fortunately for poor dear Lovie, they didn't find a thing." Beulah Jane goes over and pours herself a tall glass of tea. "What I heard is, sometimes you never can pinpoint some of those obscure poisons."

Not that I'm trying to pinpoint anything. I'm bowing out of this investigation. As soon as I find Bertha.

"Has anybody seen Bertha?" I ask.

"She's in mourning," Beulah Jane says, "I don't think she'll be coming here."

"Why, she was just here. Didn't you see her?"

Beulah Jane's face turns bright red. "Well, Tewanda, I guess I was too busy *doing my job* to be watching for widows."

"Where did you see her?" I'm eager to get on the trail, especially with a quarrel brewing between the fan club's top two officers.

"Over by stage one. Dressed in a blouse so low cut you could see everything she's got."

Looks like Bertha's cast off her widow's weeds in record time.

"What were you doing over by stage one?" Beulah Jane wants to know.

"That's where the toilets are. But then, I guess you're so high and mighty you never have to take a tinkle."

Easing out of the booth, I tell them, "Bye" but I don't think they hear me. *Holy cow.* Is that what Lovie and I will be like in thirty years? Given my choice, I'd rather be like Mama. Or even Fayrene, who at least wears an up-to-date hairdo, thanks to yours truly.

As I race toward stage one I spot two volunteers I don't know manning the T-shirt booth with Fayrene, of all people. I guess this means she's still sparring with Jarvetis. Normally, the only thing that can get her out of Gas, Grits, and Guts is an outing with Mama. And I know for a fact that Mama is at Everlasting Monuments.

Or at least, *I think* I know it for a fact. With Mama, nothing is certain.

I wave but Fayrene doesn't see me, which is just as well. She'd be full of questions, most of them nosey.

I smell Bertha before I see her. Old Mosquito Hair Spray herself is standing in the middle of the crowd around stage one talking to none other than Thaxton Miller. I reach down and pat my gun holster just to be sure it's still there, though how I think I could get by with firing a weapon in the middle of a crowd in downtown Tupelo is beyond me.

Easing closer, I scrunch down and almost knee-walk so Bertha won't see me. Being taller than the average woman is an advantage if you want everybody in a room to notice you're wearing a cute new dress with Jimmy Choo shoes, but it's a real pain if you're trying not to be seen.

I bump into an old gentleman and almost knock him off his walker.

"Excuse me," I say, but I'm too much a lady to repeat what he says. Suffice it say, I revise my opinion about him being a gentleman.

I crab-walk sideways, then risk standing up so I can see what Bertha's up to. It turns out she's up to her cleavage in rage. If I've ever seen a madder woman, I don't want to recall it. She has ditched her black coat, and her face and neck are mottled all the way down to her popping-out you know whats.

I ease closer and try to hear what she's saying, but I'm hampered by two very large women wearing *Elvis Lives!* T-shirts who form a solid wall of flesh, then glare at me as if I've tried to make off with their Social Security checks.

If I'm going to prevent Bertha from killing Thaxton, I'm going to have to adopt Lovie's *don't mess with* me attitude.

Rising to my full height, I tower a good four inches over them.

"Excuse me, please. I have to get through."

"Don't mess with me, missy." The larger of the

177

two gets right in my face. "I been here since eight o'clock this morning to hear Willie Nelson, and if you think you can be Johnny Come Lately and waltz on through, then I'm fixing to sell you a rooster that lays eggs."

Apologizing profusely, I backtrack and try to find a way around.

I guess I showed them.

Chapter 14

Sweet Talk, Lies, and Vanishing Elvises

By the time I get close enough to hear what Bertha's angry about, she's made a complete about-face and is sweet-talking Love Me Tender Elvis.

Running her hands all over Thaxton's chest and down toward dangerous regions I don't care to discuss, Bertha croons, "Now, Thaxton, you're just too precious to think such a thing about little ole me."

Somebody from Chicago or Scranton might interpret this display to mean Thaxton is the love of Bertha's life, but I'm here to tell you, it's not necessarily so. The minute a southern belle uses the word *precious,* you can bet she has not handed you a compliment. *Doris, those shoes are just so precious* is her way of saying *Those shoes are so tacky I wouldn't wear them to the pigpen.* And if a pure-blood southern belle says *Aren't you just precious?* she'd as soon cut out your liver as look at you.

Thaxton Miller is in big trouble. If I'm going to prevent his death by exotic poison, I'm going to need backup. I consider calling the police, but only briefly. What would I say to them? *I've withheld evidence that points to Bertha being the killer and now she's going to kill again?*

179

"Come on, precious," Bertha tells Thaxton. "Let's go somewhere cozy so we can kiss and make up."

She walks off with her future victim.

Holy cow! She has cajoled him toward his death. There's no time to do anything except follow them, easier said than done in this crowd. Willie Nelson is one of the few great entertainers left from the Elvis era, and three states (Mississippi, Alabama, Tennessee) have turned out in force.

Thaxton and Bertha are heading toward the east gate. Grateful for my long legs and skinny self, I step over obstacles (small dogs, empty lawn chairs, and several coolers) and slide through holes in the crowd with the ease of the Shadow, only once having to suck in my stomach so I can get through.

Bertha and her prey break out of the crowd and head toward the Bancorp South Convention Center's parking lot with me right behind them. The lot is a solid sea of vehicles, mostly SUVs and pickup trucks, and I lose them. While I'm trying to decide whether to race back to my Dodge Ram, which is parked way back up at Courthouse Square, a motorcycle roars by so fast I'd never know who was on it except for one thing: I can spot a bad hairdo a mile.

It's Bertha, jiggling all over Love Me Tender Elvis. Doesn't she know better than to get on that bike without a helmet?

I wait long enough to see them hang a left out of the parking lot and another left on Main. Bertha said *some place cozy,* and the Hilton Garden Inn where the impersonators are staying is the closest cozy spot in that direction.

I break into a run and head to my truck, congratulating myself all the way that I never slack on my fitness routine. If I did I'd be bigger than my truck, considering all the sherry-laced chocolate delights Lovie offers up.

By the time I get back to Main, Thaxton and Bertha are nowhere in sight. With only instinct as my guide, I head straight to the hotel. I don't know what I'll do when I find them. My plan is just to take one step at a time and depend on my stellar instincts for my next move.

I don't see a motorcycle in the parking lot. Have I lost them or did they transfer to Bertha's car while I was getting my truck? I don't know what she drives, so there's no way I can tell.

Since I'm here anyway I might as well find out if she's in Thaxton's room vamping him one more time before she knocks him off.

I march straight into the lobby and right up to the desk clerk, Ricky Pate, according to his name tag, an efficient-looking young man with killer looks and a wide smile. Probably smart, college educated, good family.

What is wrong with me? Lately I can't look at a member of the opposite sex between the ages of twenty-five and forty without considering his genes, and I'm not talking Levi's here.

"I'm here to see Thaxton Miller." Let Mr. Centerfold Gorgeous think whatever he wants. By the time I offer explanations, Thaxton could be dead. "Will you ring his room?"

The Pate hunk shuffles through his files. "Did you say *Thaxton Miller?*" I nod, and he says, "He checked out."

"Oh dear." South of the Mason-Dixon Line, the helpless act usually gets results. "There must be some mistake. I had a two o'clock appointment with him."

"I'm sorry, ma'am. He checked out this morning at eight."

That leaves Bertha's apartment in Magnolia Manor as the last available *cozy place* for them. Maybe I'm not too late.

As I head that way I wonder when I got old enough for twenty-year-olds to call me *ma'am.*

Finally I get lucky: there are three bikes parked in the lot, one of them Jack's Harley Screamin' Eagle. It's the only one I know because I make it my practice *not* to pay attention to motorcycle brands.

Hoping one of them belongs to Thaxton, I head through the front door. Thank goodness Jack's still in Mexico (meaning he's not here to catch me), which I refuse to dwell upon because if I do I might start agonizing *everything to do with my almost-ex* in spite of the fact I swore off worry. Since it was only a recent resolution, I don't feel bad that I can't seem to keep it.

I sashay past the manager/owner's office and barrel up the stairs two at a time (just in case the elevator breaks down and I get trapped inside, which would be my luck considering the hot air balloon episode). When I get to Bertha's apartment I can't decide whether to ring the bell or break and enter.

If I break and enter I might interrupt something I don't care to see, but if I ring the bell, I've lost the element of surprise.

Shoot, if Lovie can pick a lock, so can I. I've got everything else in my purse: I'm bound to have a hairpin.

I do, but it proves to be an uncooperative brand. After three minutes of probing, all I end up with is a broken fingernail and a bent hairpin. Since I'm not the kind of woman to let small setbacks deter me, I ring Bertha's doorbell. Naturally I'm not going to blurt out *I'm here to prevent murder.* What I'll say is, *Uncle Charlie needs to get Dick's funeral scheduled and I'm here so it'll be easier for you to make the arrangements.*

Bertha doesn't appear on the first ring, nor even the fifth. I just politely march myself downstairs and ring the doorbell on the apartment that has ERIC MILLER, MANAGER/OWNER painted on the door. I wonder if he's any relation to Thaxton.

A burly man who looks like he does serial killing on the side answers. I wish I'd had time to dress in disguise in case I make him mad and he decides to find me and slit my throat. The only thing I can do now is tell the truth—or at least enough to get me into Bertha's apartment.

I present my card from Eternal Rest that features my name below a gold-embossed butterfly, a symbol of hope, of emerging from an ordinary cocoon to become something more beautiful. The Valentines are renowned for positive attitudes and optimistic funerals, complete with a jazz band and dancing Jezebels if that's what the mourners want.

And sometimes surprise Jezebels who inherit all the money, but that's a whole other story (the Bubbles Caper).

"I'm here to make arrangements with Bertha Gerard about her husband's funeral," I tell the formidable Mr. Miller. "I rang her bell, but apparently it's broken."

"It ain't broke." He lifts an arm the size of a Virginia ham and scratches his hairy, unwashed pit. I almost pass out from the fumes. "Who did you say you was again?"

So much for showing my card. Obviously he can't read small print. I briefly consider seizing this opportunity to give a false name, then think better of it.

"Callie Valentine. From Eternal Rest Funeral Home. Dick's body is there."

"Too bad about Dick. Wonder who done it."

"I wouldn't know." I hope my eye is not twitching. Jack says it does when I lie. "I'm just here to see Bertha. Do you know if she's home?"

Mr. Miller's apartment has a picture window that faces the parking lot and a row of smaller windows on the inside facing the entry hall. The venetian blinds are wide open and a big-screen TV blares inside. The setup is the only thing that passes for security in Magnolia Manor. Not only does the manager see his tenants' comings and goings, but he also can see who else enters his building, including yours truly. Unless, of course, they use the back door.

Even if I weren't such a keen observer, I'd know all this because of Jack.

"Don't reckon she is," Mr. Two-steps-away-from-prison says. "She's gone."

"Gone?" As in *dead* or *visiting?* I'm afraid to ask.

"Yeah. Moved out without notice. If I hadn't seen the moving van at the back door, I wouldn't have knowed a thing about it."

"When was this?"

"About eighty thirty this morning. Saw it just as it was pulling out."

"Do you know where she's moving?"

"If I did I'd serve her with papers. She owes two weeks' rent."

I guess killing and stealing go together.

"Which moving company?"

185

He names one on the south side of town while I get up enough courage to ask him if he's kin to Thaxton Miller. It's a long shot, but who knows? It might be the best lead I have.

"Listen, lady, if I was kin to this Thaxton feller, I wouldn't admit it. Any man with a name that wimpy ain't got no business being a Miller."

Do you thank somebody for that kind of information, or what? While I'm trying to decide, he slams the door in my face. So much for manners.

I head to my Dodge Ram and call Lovie.

I don't make any apologies, either. Some things are worth interrupting personal business over, and murder is one of them.

"Is Rocky still there?"

Lovie says a word she didn't learn in Sunday school. Obviously the whole Calgon/bubbles/ seduction plan didn't go well.

"He said he had to go back to the motel to *take care of some details for his dig.*" She couldn't sound more scathing if fire were shooting from her nostrils. Knowing Lovie, maybe it is.

"He probably did exactly what he said. It must take lots of organization for an archaeological trip that will last months. For goodness' sake, Lovie. He sent *roses.*"

"Who are you now? Rocky's PR person?"

Ordinarily I'd say *Sarcasm doesn't become you,* but I can smell hurt all over the place, and I'm not about to add to her feeling of rejection.

"No, I'm your favorite cousin who is trying to prove you didn't kill the impersonators." I bring Lovie up to date on the poison and the escaped lovers. "You've got to help me find them before she kills him."

"I can't find Rocky's libido. How do you expect me to find Bertha and Thaxton?"

"I'm coming to get you. Be ready in ten minutes."

"In disguise?"

That's one thing I love best about Lovie, her ability to bound right back.

"No. Just put on something besides bubbles. And be ready for bribery."

I gun the engine and hightail it out of Magnolia Manor. Bertha has a huge head start. We don't have any time to lose.

Elvis' Opinion #8 on Foreign Languages, Freedom, and Illegitimate Dogs

Ruby Nell never pays the least bit of attention to what Callie tells her, which is all right with me. I like hanging out at Everlasting Monuments. People don't pop off like flies in Mooreville, so the pace is slow and lazy around here.

Even dogs live longer (the clean air and laid-back lifestyle, I guess), which suits my purposes fine. I have a big agenda, like seeing all the Valentines settled down and happy. I don't want to be hampered by having to give up my sassy basset suit and come back as something else. What if I came back as a cow? Of course, knowing my resourcefulness, I'd figure some way to get right into the middle of Valentine business, even if it meant learning to moo six bars of "Love Me Tender."

Ruby Nell's inside polishing her toenails purple and watching *Days of Our Lives*. She's partial to soaps and keeps the nineteen-inch TV in her office blaring at all times, even when customers are here. They're so distraught they don't notice, anyhow, and I've never seen a woman multitask the way Ruby Nell Valentine can. I'm probably the only one who notices she can follow every line of a soap saga while inventing creative tombstone

188

slogans like *Martha baked her way to Glory and is preparing a big banquet in the sky.*

Did I say she's also studying an Italian/English dictionary? She's gotten wind of Callie and Lovie's trip to Italy next summer, and she's not planning on being left behind.

Ditto for me, but I don't need to learn a foreign language. All I have to do is look cute and howl one of my gold hits, and I can get by in any country no matter what the natives speak.

Right now I'm sitting on the screened-in porch Ruby Nell built on the back of Everlasting Monuments so she and Fayrene can loaf and enjoy iced tea laced with whatever they're in the mood for. Usually it's lemon, but sometimes it's something stronger that would give Callie nightmares if she knew.

I'll never tell. Ruby Nell covers my back and I cover hers. She never even latches the screen on this porch because she knows dogs, like women, need their freedom.

Well, bless'a my soul. What's that over yonder behind the video store? A stray, looks like. If I don't take care of this matter, Callie will have that mutt scooped up and sitting in my yard on a satin pillow. Her strays are driving me to howl "You're the Devil in Disguise." Not to mention they're gobbling my chow and making moves on my guitar-shaped pillow.

I clump down the back steps, a heroic canine

who's not about to let a little thing like a bandage and a few narcotics stop me. I give a warning growl, which usually sends the lower class running. Not this time, in spite of the fact I've got warrior blood coursing through my veins from Morning Dove White (the King's great-great-great-grandmother). Of course, I'm so peaceable by nature I think my Cherokee heritage translated mostly as good looks.

It looks like I'm going to have to grit my teeth and drag all the way across the yard.

I'm only halfway there when the stray takes matters into his own hands and prances my way. Correct that. *Hers*. The doc's drugs have done a number on my eyesight.

Turns out the intruder is none other than my French cutie, Ann-Margret. She greets me with a haughty look and turns her back with a dismissive switch of her shapely tail.

Well, bless'a my soul. She's all knocked up and not the least bit interested in sneaking off for a good time.

Let me tell you, there's nothing like being faced with parenthood to make a smart dog stop and think. Listen, there are enough illegitimate dogs in this world. I, for one, do not intend to add to that problem.

Besides, I kind of like the idea of a mixed-breed puppy with Ann-Margret's looks and my talent and valor.

Putting on my best grin, I sashay over to my little Frenchie and ask *What's cooking, baby?*

Wrong question. She snaps at me like I stole her Pup-Peroni. Faced with female wrath, I do what any red-blooded American dog would do: I get down on my knees and beg.

I croon a few bars of "Help Me Make It through the Night," and I'm not the least bit ashamed of borrowing a song from Kris Kristofferson. This is the love of my life and it's marriage I'm talking here. And thanking my lucky stars doggie matrimony doesn't involve all that silly business with tuxedos and stale wedding cake and legal documents that don't mean a fart in a whirlwind.

Ann-Margret becomes putty in my paws. What did you expect? When I walked on two legs and had sideburns, women threw their panties at me.

My little Frenchie seals the deal with a chaste nuzzle to my heroic chest. However, she declines to share my pillow, preferring instead to maintain separate residences and see each other when it's convenient—her delicate way of saying when the heat's on and she's in the mood. I'm fine with that, as long as every other dog in the neighborhood knows to keep his paws off.

Ann-Margret trots her cute butt home and I mosey on back to the porch. I'm just getting comfortable, weaving in and out of rabbit-chasing dreams, when Charlie arrives.

I amble back inside because I don't want to miss

this. Callie's been wondering what's up between these two, but I've been knowing all along. Unearthing secrets just took a little smart detective work and a lot of eavesdropping.

Ruby Nell fixes Charlie a glass of iced tea with lemon and switches off her TV. He's the only one she does that for.

"The impersonators were poisoned," he tells her. "Security has been beefed up around the festival." He sips his tea and avoids looking at her. "I'll be glad when it's over."

"You didn't come here to discuss the festival, Charlie."

"You're right. I didn't."

He sets his glass on her desk, careful to use the tile she keeps there. *Give your soul a bubble bath,* it says. Let me tell you, that Ruby Nell knows a thing or two about living. If more people took care of their spirits and souls instead of trying to take care of everybody else's business, this world would be a better place.

"It's just dancing, Charlie."

"How did you know what I was going to say?"

"Because I know you."

"I promised my brother on his deathbed I'd take care of you. And I intend to do it, Ruby Nell, whether you like it or not."

I smell Ruby Nell's loss clear over here by the door. Her husband's deathbed was brief, the fifteen-minute ride to the hospital from the creek where his tractor plunged in, Ruby Nell and Charlie in the ambulance with him, begging him to live. I've heard this story a jillion times.

"Believe me, Charlie. I appreciate everything you've done."

They stare at each other, their silence so complete even a human without extraordinary ears could hear the baby Ben clock on her desk ticking. Finally, Ruby Nell picks up her polish and starts putting a coat of glitter over her purple-painted toenails.

"I checked up on that Whitenton guy."

"For Pete's sake, Charlie. Thomas is my *dance partner.*"

"He's had three wives, all of them rich."

"I don't want to marry him. Just boogie with him."

"Interesting choice of words, Ruby Nell."

"Okay, then. Fox-trot, salsa, tango, rumba. Take your pick. And besides that, I asked you to be my partner."

"I don't like to dance."

"You used to."

"That was a long time ago."

"Everything was a long time ago." She sets her polish aside and grabs a newspaper to fan her feet. "Did you ever wonder what our lives would be like if we'd made different choices? If I'd moved to New York after Michael died, Callie might be a famous hairdresser and I might be married."

"Is that what you want, Ruby Nell?"

"I want to *live,* Charlie."

She stands up and twirls around the room. Since there's no music, I howl a few bars of "Tennessee Waltz."

Nobody's paying attention. They're too busy with their pissing contest, Ruby Nell flaunting her daredevil independence and Charlie lobbying for caution.

He's a commanding man. Only somebody of Ruby Nell's spitfire nature could defy him. When he gets out of his chair, he just stands there till he gets her attention.

But she doesn't capitulate. Watching him out of the corner of her eye, she finishes her dance with a flirty flash of leg that flushes his cheeks, then stops right in front of his nose.

"I've scheduled us to work at the T-shirt booth tonight. Will you be there, Ruby Nell?"

"This is tango night in Pontotoc. I'll get somebody to sub for me." She grabs his hands. "Come with me, Charlie. Live a little. Be wild and crazy."

When Ruby Nell starts to cajole, it's not easy to turn her down. Ask Callie. Ruby Nell wrote the book on charm. And for a woman her age—or any age for that matter—she's a real looker.

I can see Charlie's turmoil. Somewhere inside him is still the man who could take Bourbon Street by storm, start out the night with a dollar in his pocket and end up buying drinks for everybody at Pat O'Brian's. Of course, that was the good old days when his sap was high and the levee was holding.

I strike up a few bars of "Are You Lonesome Tonight?" hoping Charlie will get the message. No sense in a good-looking, kindhearted man like him sitting in his apartment above Eternal Rest reading Shakespeare when he could be out having some fun.

Much as I admire and love him, I'll have to side with Ruby Nell this time. If you can't loosen up and live a little, what's the use of living at all?

Charlie just grabs his hat and walks out.

Looks like I've got more work cut out for me than I thought.

Chapter 15

Bribery, Cute Shoes, and Dark and Deadly Strangers

Lovie is waiting for me on her front porch, carrying a cake and wearing a skirt so short there's a bare inch between imagination and the real thing. She's also wearing a pair of sling black Kate Spade heels I'd envy if I weren't above it. At least with my cousin.

"Where are your boots, Lovie?"

Instead of answering, she settles into the passenger seat. "Gun it, Callie. Let's get out of this neighborhood." She proceeds to stick her foot over on my side of the truck toward the accelerator.

"For Pete's sake." I whack her with the only weapon handy, a half-eaten box of Cracker Jack. "What's gotten into you?"

"Nothing. As you well know."

"Maybe that's a good thing."

"No, it's not. Rocky and I have been dating long enough to move to the next level. Something must be wrong. I've never met a man I couldn't seduce."

"And how many of those men ever sent you roses? Or flew all the way across the country just to sit on the sofa and hold your hand? Or bothered to stick around long enough to find out you're worthy of more than a roll in the hay?"

She's quiet—thinking it over, I hope, or else admiring the view of her quaint neighborhood. Several years ago it was going to rack and ruin, but new owners came in and started an aggressive campaign of gentrification. Now the neighborhood looks much the same as it did when Elvis (the King, not my dog) attended Milam School two blocks from Lovie's house.

"What's the cake for?" I ask her.

"You'll see."

We cross Main Street, then head south on Church. When I pull into the parking lot of Trouble-Free Movers, I don't have a single idea how I'm going to extract private information about Bertha.

"Wait here," Lovie says, then bails out.

I'm relieved to sit back and let somebody else do the dirty work. If any more intimidating Eric Millers and mouthwatering Ricky Pates are around, let Lovie deal with them for a change. Besides, she needs something to take her mind off Rocky and his stalled libido.

Don't let it be dead, that's all I ask. For Lovie's sake, let him be a normal, red-blooded male who just happens to believe in the old-fashioned ideals of courtship and marriage.

By the time she gets back I've solved all her problems (only in my mind, of course) and she's happily married with three children. If only it were that easy to solve my own.

Lovie climbs into my Dodge Ram, sans cake, and I ask, "Did you find out anything?"

"Bertha's furniture is on its way to Las Vegas."

The city where Lovie mooned half its residents and we nearly got caught breaking and entering. I don't hanker to go there again.

"She's probably heading that way, too," I say. "With Thaxton."

"Which means if she's going to kill him, she'll have plenty of time before we catch up with her."

"Are you suggesting we trail them to Las Vegas?"

Lovie says a word that would embarrass sailors. "Do I look like I rolled off the watermelon truck? If you think I'm fixing to haul across the desert just so I can be near another dead Elvis, you're not as smart as I give you credit for."

"Bertha will have to come back sometime," I say. "Or at least call."

"Why?"

"They've released her husband's body. It's at Uncle Charlie's and Bertha didn't leave funeral instructions. Poor Dick."

"Maybe she doesn't care what we do with him."

"Shoot. What a mess."

Now I'm going to have to tell Uncle Charlie about Bertha's move and he'll know I went sleuthing against his wishes. Not that he'll get mad. Or if he does, I'll never know it. I could prob-ably race to the top of the Statue of Liberty and

198

moon New York and Uncle Charlie would just say *now, now, dear heart.*

Lovie and I sit in my Dodge Ram in ninety-degree heat with the motor idling and the air conditioner running on high while I try to think of a next move that will keep us on the track but out of trouble. Not an easy task.

"How'd you get the movers to give you Bertha's forwarding address?" I ask her.

"You don't want to know."

"Yes, I do."

"Combine chocolate with a few seductive moves and you can get just about anything you want." Leave it to Lovie. "If Rocky were that easy I'd be sitting in the catbird seat."

"Don't give me that. If he were that easy you wouldn't have him. Not on any permanent basis."

"Who says I'm thinking about permanence?"

"Well, aren't you?"

"Maybe." Lovie fiddles with the radio till she finds a station that plays blues. "With our prime suspect gone, looks like we're up doodoo creek without a paddle."

"Not necessarily. We were wrong about George. What if we're on the wrong track with Bertha?"

"I'm never on the wrong track." Lovie licks a bit of chocolate icing off her finger. "Sometimes I need to make a little correction, that's all."

"Let's switch our focus from motive to means

and see what we can find out." I back out of the parking lot and head downtown.

"Where are we going?"

"Reed's Bookstore. While we're this close we might as well grab everything we can find on exotic poisons."

"The toxicologists don't even know what kind it was, Callie."

"I'm not saying we can pinpoint the poison, but if we have some general idea of what it might be and where it came from, maybe we can work backward and discover who would have access."

"That's a lot of big maybes," she says.

"I can't just sit by while you're accused of poisoning Elvises."

"Lead on, Sherlock. It's not as if I have anything exciting to occupy me this afternoon."

Which means she's not seeing Rocky. I'm not going to ask, but I do strike a little silent bargain with God that if He'll smooth the romantic path for my cousin, I'll clean out my closet and give my excess cute designer shoes to deserving people. But only the shoes I've already worn at least twice.

At the bookstore, I try to look natural (translation: not up to something) while I browse among the books on poison. I'm standing behind the racks in a semisquat so nobody can see me over the top when Lovie brays, "Come over here and look at this book on gardening, Callie. It has a whole page about poison mushrooms."

She doesn't know the meaning of discreet.

Everybody on my side of the stacks turns to stare, including Clytee Estes. Who outranks Fayrene in the gossip department. And she's an officer of the Tupelo Elvis Fan Club. The only thing worse would have been Jack standing there.

I lurch upright and hurry over to Lovie. "Would you keep it down? What do you want, everybody in Tupelo on the witness stand telling how you were in the bookstore looking for books on poison?"

"Let 'em talk. It won't be the first time."

As a matter of fact, it won't. Lovie's a colorful character and makes no bones about it. Last Christmas she was at the center of a swirling controversy when she was tapped for the church pageant as the Virgin Mary. Fannie Jo Franks, who has been lobbying for the role all year, started the rumor Lovie got it because she went to the auditions wearing a blouse cut down to her navel. Lovie finally put an end to the rumor by saying she was typecast.

It's hard to spread vicious gossip when you're laughing.

Still, *researching poisons* is one bit of gossip I want to keep away from Lovie's door.

All of a sudden I remember the movie *White Oleander* where Michelle Pfeiffer's character poisoned her lovers with the beautiful but lethal tropical flower. Maybe Lovie has a point about poison mushrooms.

201

I snatch up some gardening books without even looking at the titles, add them to the stack I've already selected, then hustle over to checkout before I get arrested as an accomplice to murder.

Back at Lovie's cottage I call to check on Elvis.

"He's sound asleep." Mama sounds out of breath.

"What are you doing, Mama?"

"Just whirling around a bit. Practicing my tango steps."

"By yourself?"

"No, Elvis is here. And Thomas."

Bound for Mama. She knows good and well I won't chastise her about not taking Elvis straight home to bed because she's just dropped a bomb-shell.

"He wouldn't be the little *something* that came up over in Tunica, would he, Mama?"

"I don't recall giving you the third degree when you were dating."

"You're *dating?*" Lovie starts laughing and I stick out my tongue. "Mama, why do you keep secrets like this? If you're seeing somebody I have a right to know."

"You sound like Charlie. Act your age, Callie. Last time I looked it wasn't eighty-five. Ta-tah."

Mama hangs up. I'm in the midst of calling her right back when Lovie says, "For Pete's sake, Callie. Let Aunt Ruby Nell alone. At least some-body in this family is having fun."

"You don't think she'd elope without telling me?"

"I don't."

"How can you be so sure?"

"Because I know Aunt Ruby Nell. If she ever walks down the aisle again, she'll have a brass band and a parade of exotic dancing girls following her to the altar."

I pick up the first book on our stash from Reed's, which just happens to be a book on gardening.

"Do I act eighty-five, Lovie?"

"Sometimes." I'm going to kill her. "But mostly you're my gorgeous, talented, young-at-heart best friend who just happens to be my cousin."

Okay, so I'll let her live.

Still stewing about Mama, I flip through the gardening book without expecting to see a thing. Lovie is digging through *Forensics for Dummies* and a box of chocolate-covered cherries.

She pops two into her mouth and tosses two to me. I nibble the chocolate off one side, then suck out the juice, saving the cherry for last. Sometimes there's comfort in calories.

"According to this," she says, "there's no such thing as an untraceable poison. Which means we're spinning our wheels over something the toxicologist will eventually find out."

I'm only half listening because I've stumbled over a pure gold mine. Not evidence, exactly, but a lead I would never have dreamed.

"*Eventually* is the key, Lovie. While the experts

are still looking, we can nab the killer. Listen to this. *Plants that may cause death.* Creamy poison milk vetch, death camas, mountain laurel, castor bean, common tansy, lily of the valley. And that's just the tip of the iceberg. Holy cow!"

If this list is not *exotic poisons,* I don't know what is. It looks like we're on to something.

"Lovie, find everything you can about these plants, where they're grown, how they kill, where you'd get their poison oils, and so forth."

"What are you going to do?"

"I have to go to Eternal Rest and fix up poor dead Dick. Call me when you find out anything that stands out."

"I'm not speaking to you again if you don't stop calling him *poor dead Dick.*"

"Listen, Lovie. I don't think Rocky's *you know what* is dead. I just think he's saving it."

"For what? The second coming?" Trust Lovie to tangle up sex and religion. And who knows? Maybe they ought to be. There were times when sex with Jack was a religious experience. Sometimes I'd think *if this is not the closest thing to experiencing the wonder of the universe, I don't know what is.*

Let me get out of here before I get converted to hedonism or something. Lovie's pink house tends to do that to me, work some kind of voodoo magic. Frankly, I don't see how Rocky can come here and resist.

• • •

Uncle Charlie is not at the funeral home. "Gone fishing," Bobby Huckabee tells me. I'm glad. This lets me off the hook about telling him Bertha's whereabouts and gives Uncle Charlie a chance to relax. It also gives me an opportunity to get to know his assistant better.

Bobby is painfully homely and shy, especially with me, but he's very good at his job. Otherwise, Uncle Charlie would never have hired him, let alone left him in charge of Eternal Rest.

"The body's downstairs," he says, then scoots back about four feet and stands there jiggling his left leg. This is the equivalent of a schoolboy shuffling his feet, bursting with something else to say but uncertain whether to blurt it out or run.

"Was there something else, Bobby?"

"Well, I thought I'd go down to keep you company. If that's all right with you. I don't want to impose."

"I'm always glad to have company. My clients at Eternal Rest aren't exactly a barrel of laughs."

His messy guffaw is all out of proportion to my joke. *Poor Bobby. Trying too hard to please.*

I put my arm through his and let him escort me down the stairs. I'm determined to do everything I can to put him at ease.

"It's wonderful to have you here, Bobby. After you get to know us better, I hope you'll think of us as family."

"Oh, I already do with your mama."

See, that's the reason Mama can get away with so much. She's so charming nobody can resist her. Correct that. She's charming when she wants to be.

"Most folks don't take to me right away on account of my psychic eye, but Ruby Nell says it's one of my biggest assets."

Psychic eye? Bobby turns to show me the other side of his face.

"It's this blue one. It lets me see things."

Maybe he can *see* who murdered the impersonators. As nervous as he is, I don't want to scare him away. I'll have to broach that subject gradually.

Soft pink light spills from the wall sconces with their shell-shaped shades. The dead deserve respect and Uncle Charlie has made sure this room is as uplifting and beautiful as possible.

While I open my makeup kit, Bobby plops onto the end of the sofa where Uncle Charlie usually sits.

When I start with Dick I can't get the image out of my head of him slumped on my patio with his swivel permanently stilled. This is my first murder victim to prepare for the great heareafter, and let me tell you, there's a big difference between working on a corpse who died peacefully and one who was murdered. It seems to me Dick's spirit is not resting easy. It's almost like he's vibrating under my touch, trying to rise up and tell me something. Probably who killed him.

I'm grateful Bobby's in the room.

Out of the blue he says, "I see wheels on the horizon."

"What?"

I glance over and he's sitting so straight and still he looks like a cardboard imitation of himself. The way he's staring into the distance is eerie, and I whirl around to look behind my back, half expecting to see somebody there. Carrying a butcher knife.

Or a flacon of poison.

"Wheels. For you. A new sports car. Red." He rolls his blue eye, but not the green. How does he do that? "I see travel, lots of events, picnics, and weddings, you'll be attending weddings."

I rethink my decision to involve Bobby in the murder case. There's no way I'm trading my big Dodge pickup for a car that's low slung and wimpy, one that doesn't have the muscle to say *I'm bad to the bone, back off.* As for travel and social events, that could be part of anybody's future.

"Wait!" Suddenly Bobby turns his blue eye on me, and it's like being hit by a blast of air-conditioning. I wrap my arms around myself to keep from shivering.

"I'm getting something." His voice is low and urgent. Between Bobby and Dick I'm wondering who turned this tranquil mostly pink room I love into a spook house.

"Something big," he says, and I just hope it's not Jack. Which goes to show the alarming turns a woman's mind will take when she's still halfway over the moon with her almost-ex.

"There's danger all around you," Bobby says.

I'm about to be spooked.

"Danger from a dark-eyed stranger."

Wait a minute. Right after Bobby came here, didn't I hear Mama and Fayrene discussing something about *danger from a dark-eyed stranger?*

Since the killer is focusing on impersonators, the only danger I'm likely to be in is from Elvis, who will get mad and do no telling what when I leave him home this evening while I go to the festival finale.

I don't care what Mama thinks. As far as I'm concerned, if Bobby Huckabee wants to be part of the Valentine family, he's going to have to curb his enthusiasm for predicting the future.

I finish Dick as quickly as I can. Fortunately Bobby has *seen* all he's going to and sits on the sofa without saying another word until I'm ready to leave.

"Be careful," is all he says, and I tell him I will.

It will be a relief to get into my truck and go home.

Something's flapping on my windshield. It can't be a parking ticket. I'm on the Eternal Rest lot.

I pluck the note off and unfold it.

Keep your nose out of my business or you could

be next, signed with a shaky drawing of skull and crossbones.

I let out a little yelp, but stop myself before it becomes a full-fledged scream. I'm trying to turn myself into a woman to be reckoned with.

Tucking the note into my pocket, I resolve to rethink my opinion about Bobby and his ominous predictions. As I head home I look every which way for a dark-eyed stranger, or at least somebody with a suspicious look and a beef against me. I don't cotton to the idea of being the Elvis Festival killer's next victim.

Even if I wouldn't be caught dead in a sequined jumpsuit. No pun intended.

Chapter 16

Boogie, Bad Karma, and Hot Bodies

As much as I'd love to go home and sink into a hot bubble bath, I head straight to Everlasting Monuments to rescue my dog. Wouldn't you know? Mama has stuck a CLOSED sign on the door, and it's not even closing time.

Fortunately, she doesn't have to keep regular hours. She has made the monument company so popular that people are willing to wait just so they can honor their dearly departed with a headstone from Ruby Nell Valentine. Of course, she sells great-quality stone—pink marble from Italy and black from Africa as well as the traditional gray granite.

But it's those crazy carvings that draw the crowd. *Woody's gone to the Eternal Dairy Barn to take care of the Master's cows* and *Pete's still growing prize tomatoes at that great Farmers' Market in the sky.*

Mama's sayings give the bereaved something to latch on to. I can imagine them going home and saying to each other, "Herbert, I feel better knowing Daddy's still growing tomatoes," and Herbert replying, "Yep, Izzy Mae. If Ms. Valentine carves it in stone, it has to be true."

Mama's car's not here, but I rattle the knob and

bang on the door just in case she and Fayrene are carpooling. They do that sometimes when they have plans for the evening, pick each other up way in advance, drop one car off, then take care of business till it's time to leave for their latest entertainment.

My racket brings Alice Ann Street, who owns the video store next door. She prides herself on knowing the movie tastes of every one of her customers and being on hand to personally make recommendations.

"Your mama's not here, Callie."

"Do you know where she is?"

That would be a crazy question to ask in Boston or Berkeley, but in Mooreville everybody knows everybody else's business. Which is a good thing if you're sick with flu and the neighbors are waiting in your front yard with chicken soup by the time you get home from the doctor. On the other hand, it can be aggravating if you don't want anybody to know your almost-ex is still keeping your body hot. Not to mention your bed.

"A little while ago she went tearing off toward Gas, Grits, and Guts."

"Elvis was with her, I assume." I hope.

Alice Ann tells me he was, and I tear off in that direction myself. If anything else goes amiss today, I'm likely to pack my clothes and spend the night in Reed's shoe department. There's nothing like the smell of expensive leather to perk me up.

I park my Dodge Ram in front right by Mama's telltale red convertible and hurry inside. Jarvetis is behind the counter looking grim. Well, no wonder, after that stunt Mama and Fayrene pulled over in Tunica. I buy a bag of chips and a Coke, then stand there asking what he thinks about Mississippi State's baseball team, hoping that will cheer him up. The only thing Jarvetis Johnson likes better than the Bulldog baseball team is his redbone hound, Trey.

"Lately, I haven't had time to keep up with anything except Fayrene."

Jarvetis has said this before, but always with a wink and a grin. I hate to think Mama is partially the cause of this unhappy turn of events. Still, I don't want anybody blaming her.

Except me, of course.

"Is Mama in the break room?"

He nods toward the back and I head that way. I don't know what I expected, probably the jingle of quarters and the shuffling of cards. Certainly not Mama and Fayrene bent over a piece of paper with their heads together, whispering. And most certainly not them jumping when they see me, then rolling up the paper like it's a treasure map I've come to steal.

I don't even want to know what they're plotting now. Well, I do, but after the kind of day I've had I don't think I can stand any more nasty surprises. And if they're whispering so Jarvetis won't hear, the surprise is bound to be unpleasant.

They greet me like I'm a long-lost favorite relative. Confirmation they're planning trouble.

"I guess you've come to get your dog," Mama says.

If she turns the wattage of her smile up one more notch, she's going to light up Mooreville. Meanwhile, Elvis knocks the paper out of Fayrene's hand and she jerks it up and stuffs it in a cookie jar as if I don't have good eyesight and good sense, to boot.

Ordinarily I'd scold Elvis, but today I'm more concerned about his health than his manners. I scoop him up and check him out. He seems all right. His bandage hasn't been gnawed off and he's not addled. I can breathe a bit now.

I turn my attention toward my latest problem. "Is everything all right, Mama?"

"If things were any better I'd be turning cartwheels."

This could mean she and Uncle Charlie have patched up their differences or it could mean Mama's putting on a show so I won't worry. She's good at that. When I was growing up, I never knew when she cried about losing Daddy or trying to learn how to run a business, or that she worried I'd turn out wrong because I didn't have a father. It was only after I married and was furious at what I considered Mama's meddling that Jack told me those things.

"She just wants the best for you," he'd said.

I can see that so clearly now. She was always my cheerleader, my solace, my biggest fan, even my clown. Who needed a circus when you had Mama tap-dancing you around the kitchen singing "Side by Side"? In Mary Jane tap shoes she'd painted gold and then glued with sequins, no less.

"Thanks for taking care of Elvis." I give her a hug, and Fayrene, too. Listen, sometimes the best thing that happens to you all day is a hug. The nice thing is that when you give one, you get one right back.

Feeling like a better human being, I head home with my dog, leaving Mama and Fayrene to their own devices. They're grown women and they're both smart. Whatever is eating Jarvetis, they'll figure out how to handle it.

It feels so good to walk into my house, I consider sinking into a bubble bath and spending the rest of the evening in my tub. First, though, I have to see what the blinking light on my answering machine is all about. I put Elvis down and watch to see that he's walking right before I punch MESSAGES.

A deep voice says my name.

I know this man. The first big surprise is that he called; the second, that he jolts me into a state of excitement.

"This is Champ," his message tells me, as if my baby factory is not already sitting up taking notice. "I'm calling to see how Elvis is doing. I'll be at the office till seven."

I glance at my watch. He's still there.

"If you get this message, please let me know. I like to keep up with my patients."

Did he add that last to cover his real intentions? Or is he telling the truth and I'm letting my father-of-the-future-baby search make a fool of me.

Elvis clumps by wagging his tail, and I take that as a sign. Before I change my mind, I dial the number on my caller ID.

"Champ here."

"I got your message. About Elvis."

"How is he?"

"He's doing great. He's not so wobbly now and he seems to have suffered no ill effects from the medication."

"Good." There's a long pause and for a minute I think the connection is broken. I'm getting ready to hang up when he says, "You're just a few miles up the road. I can pop by tonight and check him out. If you'd like."

I imagine Champ in my house sitting on my sofa with his long legs stretched out, his big gentle hands holding a cup of green tea chai and me in the wing chair thinking that any man who fits so well in the room might fit nicely into my life.

Hard on the heels of that delightful dream I see Jack on the same sofa with his hands elsewhere and me with my skirt over my head thinking *yes, yes, yes*.

I will *not* let Jack Jones sabotage my future.

"Did you say something?" Champ asks.

Holy cow. Did I? If so, it would have been a very unladylike growl.

"Just clearing my throat. Thank you for offering, but I'll be at the Elvis Festival tonight."

After I hang up I wonder if I turned Champ down because of the festival or because of Jack. I'm not even going to think about it. Instead I call Lovie.

"Did you find out anything about the poisons?"

"Rocky's here." Lovie sounds out of breath. I'd be jealous if I were that type. "We'll talk about it at the festival tonight. Meet us at the T-shirt booth."

"When?"

"Eight?"

"Fine," I tell her in a way that clearly means the opposite.

After I hang up I ask Elvis, "How are we going to discuss poison with him around? I thought Rocky wanted her to keep her nose out of murder."

Not only am I turning surly as my eggs shrivel, but I'm also turning into one of those maidenly women who talk mostly to their cats and dogs.

I stomp outside to feed my menagerie, notice the crime scene tape still around my courtyard, and decide on the spot to name the cats. All seven of them. I need something to restore my sense that my home is a place of deep comfort and magical promise.

While dogs are great companions and protectors, it's the cats that make a place both cozy and mystical.

"All righty, then. You're Sleepy, Sneezy, Dopey, Doc, Grumpy, Bashful, Happy."

Why not? I've instantly turned my life into a fairy tale. They can be the seven dwarfs who adore me and I can be Snow White, who hopefully will not get felled by a poisoned apple. Or any other kind of poisoned plant.

Elvis stops eating, gives me his Ruby Nell look, and walks away. In time, he'll warm up to the cats.

The young champagne-colored Siamese female I've named Happy prances over to rub against my legs, then leaps around with such joie de vivre she reminds me of my college roommate, Happy Jacques, who studied dance and electrified her audience every time she went onstage.

She used to say, "Callie, there are three international languages—love, laughter, and music." I believe that.

When my newly adopted cat does a pirouette, then winks at me, I call Elvis.

"Have you been talking to this cat about reincarnation?"

I swear the Siamese is watching me with Happy Jacques' knowing eyes.

After giving my dogs and cats a quick cuddle, I go inside, take a quick shower, and change into a blue jean skirt and Elvis T-shirt before heading to the festival. As a concession to fashion I'm wearing a pair of Dolce & Gabbana flats and as a nod to murder I'm wearing my gun, strapped high on my thigh, the holster hidden under my skirt.

I pride myself on being prepared.

Elvis' Opinion #9 on Marriage, Pickled Pigs' Lips, and Mark Twain

Callie has gone off without me and I blame the cats. If she hadn't been so busy giving that bunch of silly strays names, I could have sweet-talked her into letting me attend the festival's finale.

And don't get me started on the names. If she was going to elevate them from interlopers to household members, the least she could have done was name them after some of my backup musicians like she did with Hoyt. I'd have been satisfied if she'd named a couple of them Jerry Lee Lewis and Frank Sinatra, even if old Blue Eyes did once call rock 'n' roll the music of every sideburned delinquent on the face of the earth. Years later he changed his tune and called me the embodiment of the whole American culture. I can live with that.

What I can't live with is a bunch of feline freaks. Callie had better not even think of getting little snobby cat beds and moving them in with me. If she does I'll just go live with Jarvetis. There's a man who appreciates his dogs. Not a cat on the premises.

Why do you think I was able to walk away from my supper dish tonight? Jarvetis slipped me a bunch of pickled pigs' lips when Ruby Nell carried me over there. That's what.

And speaking of tonight's visit, Ruby Nell and Fayrene's latest scheme is a doozie, but I'm not fixing to betray their confidence. All I'm going to say is this: if they go through with this project, it could be the death of marriage as Fayrene knows it.

Because Jarvetis is so easygoing, she's making the mistake of thinking she can get by with anything short of infidelity and murder. I tried to tell her every man has his limits. The trick is knowing what they are.

Jarvetis has never missed a Sunday at Bougefala Baptist Church. That ought to tell her it won't do to mess around with his religion. She got around him about going off dancing with Ruby Nell, but if she's going to get this scheme past him, it'll take a miracle.

Of course, you're looking at a miracle worker. I'll think of something.

Don't get me wrong. I care about those two, but I'm no paper saint. If Jarvetis walks I'll lose his pickled pigs' lips and his redbone hound dog, to boot.

I have lots of planning to do. I snarl at the cats, then amble toward the doggie door for some quiet cogitation on my pillow.

Wouldn't you know? Hoyt's dragged his pillow around to my side of the bed. Now he's looking at me with his silly grin that melts Callie's soft heart. But it just pisses me off.

I'm fixing to scare him off with a wild rendition of "T-R-OU-B-L-E," but then I get this great idea. (Naturally, I'm full of them.)

"Hoyt, old buddy. How'd you like to have the most fun of your young life?"

He jumps up wagging his tail so hard he's shaking his silly self all over. This is going to be easier than Tom Sawyer talking the neighborhood kids into whitewashing his fence. (Don't think I don't know my Mark Twain. I'm a dog of letters.)

As an added bonus, my plan will get Hoyt in a heap of trouble with my human mom. (Notice, I didn't say *his mom.)*

"Listen, old pal. If you could dig a little hole under the fence, I'd take you out on the town, introduce you to that cute shih tzu down the street."

Hoyt's about to wet his scraggly britches.

It's not this hyper little pest and that pain-in-the-butt down the road I have on my mind, but a certain lush Frenchie in the family way.

"I'd do the digging myself, but my paw's all banged up."

Now I've got his sympathy. Always a good thing. By the time I head toward the doggie door, Hoyt's drooling all over himself with the notion of being the King's right-hand dog.

Chapter 17

Bathroom Breaks, Hunks, and Suspicious Minds

There are more police uniforms than sequined jumpsuits at the festival tonight. That would make me feel safer if I didn't have a sinking feeling that in addition to preventing another homicide, the cops came to keep an eye on their prime suspect.

Who is not here yet. I just hope Lovie's reasons for being late mean she and Rocky have settled their differences.

Uncle Charlie is manning the T-shirt booth with Mabel Moffett and her daughter Trixie. (I guess Mama talked them into taking her place.) In spite of the fact that Lovie's an inch from being arrested, he looks his usual tranquil self. It's hard to think of him as ever having lived on the edge of the law. (That's what Lovie says about her daddy, but she could be exaggerating. She loves to embellish.)

When he sees me, he comes around and kisses my cheek.

"You look tired, dear heart. Why don't you go home? I can finish out the festival without you."

"I'm fine, Uncle Charlie. Did you catch any fish?"

"Three catfish. They made a nice supper. Bobby ate with me."

I make a mental note to invite Uncle Charlie over for dinner the minute I get this murder solved. Maybe before. Usually Mama is the one making a big pot of soup with corn bread and having impromptu Valentine get-togethers, but she's so busy going on secret dates with unknown elements she's forgotten she has a family who has her best interests at heart.

"Jack's flying home," Uncle Charlie tells me, and I'm too polite to say *I don't recall asking*. But I do ask about his health. Out of curiosity.

Okay, so I have other motives, but I'm too busy to feel guilty about it.

"There's no permanent damage," Uncle Charlie says, "but he'll be stiff for a while."

Jack's always stiff. I nearly say it aloud. I don't know why I have this die-hard attraction to a man who chooses bullets and a Harley over hearth and home. Not that I'm going to be too hard on myself. Most people want what they can't have.

But I'm planning to change. Really, I am. The minute I'm free I'm taking the cats to Champ's clinic to be fixed, and if he asks me out, I'm saying yes.

Seven cats are all right, but thirty-five are not. If anybody's going to populate this world, it's going to be me. I hope.

Lovie and Rocky arrive all cozied up. A good sign for them. On the other hand, if he's going to be glued to her side, I don't see how we're going to do any sleuthing.

I know. I'm being surly. What I ought to be is happy. Rocky and Uncle Charlie are shaking hands and exchanging niceties while Lovie watches with the deep satisfaction of a wayward daughter who has finally mended her ways and brought home a man who lives up to her daddy's expectations.

Uncle Charlie waves us off with "Have fun," which is not the reason I'm here.

As soon as we're out of his sight I tell Rocky and Lovie, "Excuse me. I have to take a little break."

She gets the picture. "I'll be back in a minute, darling."

"Take your time, sweetheart."

I don't know whether to laugh or cry. Actually, I feel like doing both. After all this is over, I'm taking a vacation.

As we head to the Porta Potti I figure nobody will pay us any attention in this crowd, so I just haul off and ask Lovie what she found out about the poison.

"Many cause convulsions, then death, and most of the oils are extracted by steam distillation."

"Which means it would take special equipment."

"Exactly. Also, the process could be dangerous.

224

I don't think we're talking about an amateur here."

"A professional hit man?"

"Maybe," she says. "Or it could be a scientist."

"What kind of scientist would want to kill Elvises?"

My question earns us some suspicious looks, so I grab Lovie's arm, drag her into the Porta Potti, and slam the door.

She says a word that uncurls my pubic hair.

"How do you expect to use the toilet with us wedged in here like sardines?"

"I don't have to use the toilet, Lovie. That was just an excuse to get you away from Rocky."

"Well, I do. Scrunch against the corner and don't move."

As she squats over the throne, the entire Porta Potti teeters toward the left. I make a quick move to the right and step on both her feet. She says another word, but I don't apologize.

"If I hadn't moved we'd have turned the toilet over."

I can just see the headlines. *Valentine Cousins Foul Festival.*

Lovie jiggles around trying to pull up her underwear, but it's too crowded in here, so she just kicks them off and leaves them on the floor.

"I don't plan on needing them, anyhow," she says, and I give her this *look.* "No, Callie, Rocky hasn't found the holy grail yet, but he's flying out tomorrow and I don't intend for him to leave without a glimpse of glory. Tonight I'm drawing him a map."

When we finally emerge, an Amazonian woman with a bad bleach job and pursed lips is standing outside the Porta Potti. She gives us the once-over, stomps inside, then yells, "Jezebels" and slams the door in our faces.

"Do you think she knows who we are, Lovie?"

"What does it matter? If we don't find the killer, my name will be in every newspaper in the world."

She's right. Elvis always made headlines, and the death of the impersonators has already made news as far away as Japan.

"Maybe one of the other impersonators is a scientist or a doctor, Lovie."

"Yeah, or maybe it's just an ordinary person who ordered the poison."

"From where?"

"South America. Central America. Who knows? You can find about anything you want on the Internet."

"That leads us back to square one," I say. "Anybody at the festival could have bought a hot dog or lemonade, laced it with poison, and passed it to one of the impersonators."

"You forget who had the biggest motive, Callie."

"Bertha. Whose furniture is headed toward Las Vegas."

"Yes, but is she?"

Lovie's right. What if I was on the wrong track with Bertha? While I was checking out her apartment and Thaxton's hotel, she could have taken him to some deserted place and killed him. His body could be lying in a remote neck of the woods anywhere in northeast Mississippi. It could take weeks to find it. Maybe years.

What if she's lurking somewhere looking for her next victim? Even worse, what if she put the threatening note on my Dodge Ram and I'm next on her list?

When I tell Lovie about the note and my suspicions that Bertha's out to get me, she says, "Not while I'm around, she won't."

My cousin grabs me and heads toward Rocky like a heat-seeking missile. I'll have to say I'm relieved. If you wanted two bodyguards, you couldn't do better than a hundred and ninety pounds of don't-mess-with-me woman and a man who looks like he could bench-press Texas.

Rocky smiles when he sees us and reaches a long arm to draw Lovie close.

"Grab a hold of Callie and don't let go," she tells him, and he obeys without question. "Somebody's trying to kill her."

"We don't know that." My protest doesn't hold much force. For one thing, I'm smothered in what feels like a side of beef (a kindly side of beef), and for another, I feel safer than I've felt since Jack left.

"Who's after her?"

"A short dishwater-blond woman with a bad hairdo and too much cleavage," Lovie says, and I have to giggle. Lovie's showing the Pike's Peak of cleavage. And always does. "Go ahead and giggle," she says. "There are women who know how to look classy flaunting it and women who look just plain cheap."

"You're right, sweetheart."

"I know, Rocky. I'm always right. I'm also starving. Let's have a corn dog on a stick."

"Do you think that's wise, Lovie?" I'm starving, too, having had very little to eat today and most of that on the run. But I'm not about to take chances eating at the festival when we don't have any idea who's poisoning what.

"They fry those things in hot grease while you watch," she says.

"Not always," I tell her. "Sometimes the corn dogs are already on a spit."

"We'll ask for fresh," Rocky says, and that settles that.

Lovie and I haul off in that direction, flanking Rocky like glued-on bookends. Within smelling distance of the deep-fried food, I change my mind.

"I think I'll have one, too," I'm saying when a scream comes from the direction of stage one. We whirl around and Lovie and I spot Bertha at the same time.

228

"There she is," says Lovie, and Rocky sprints that way, calling back over his shoulder, "Stay put."

"It'll take more than Bertha Gerard to separate me from food." Lovie marches me up to the stand and orders three large lemonades and five corn dogs on a stick. I don't have to ask. One for me, two for her, two for Rocky.

Six are laid out under the warming lamp. When the vendor reaches for them, Lovie says, "No. I want fresh. And I want to see them cooking."

There's a tense, slow-motion moment when Lovie and the vendor stare at each other like cowboys daring to see who will draw his six-shooter first. Finally, the vendor shrugs, opens a fresh package of hot dogs, and starts cooking.

I never doubted that Lovie would win.

There's still a commotion going on by the stage. I'm torn between craning my neck to find out what's happening and keeping an eye on the food to make sure nobody slips in some exotic poison. Since the crowd by the stage is not growing larger and the screaming has stopped, I opt for vendor surveillance.

When somebody touches me on the shoulder from behind, I nearly jump out of my skin.

"I'm sorry. I didn't mean to startle you."

Holy cow! It's Champ, all golden and freshly scrubbed. If you want to know the truth, he's a hunk. Wouldn't you know my tail's dragging and my shoes are dusty? Thank goodness they're cute. The only thing that would make me feel better is a little spritz of Jungle Gardenia on my pulse points. Just in case.

Lovie turns around and I tell her, "You remember Dr. Luke Champion?"

When her right eyebrow shoots up, I brace myself for one of her ribald comments, but all she says is, "Of course. I'm Lovie Valentine. I brought Callie's dog to see you earlier in the summer."

"I remember. Is it thanks to you I have a new patient?"

"Yes." The vendor passes Lovie's order across the counter and she tells Champ, "We're having corn dogs. Join us."

She offers one to him, then nudges me in the ribs, which means *here's your chance, grab it,* though how I'm going to seize opportunity, catch a killer, worry over Mama's secret boyfriend, and hide the fact that I'm wearing a gun all at the same time is beyond me. Still, chaos is no reason to let manners slip.

"By all means, if you don't have other plans, please join us. Lovie's friend Rocky will be back soon."

"Thanks." When Champ accepts the corn dog I get goose bumps, which I take as a sign. Of what, I don't know. It could be good or bad, but the way I feel standing next to him, I'm betting it's good.

230

"Actually," he says, smiling straight at me, "I was hoping to find you here."

In spite of circumstances, I get warm and fuzzy. Of course, I felt the same way when Jack first took notice of me. Well, maybe not warm and fuzzy. More like a Fourth of July fireworks explosion.

I believe in fate. The universe put Champ in my path for a purpose. I'm standing here smiling, trying to figure out if the purpose is what I want it to be (you don't even have to ask). At the same time, I'm trying to figure out how Lovie and I can carry out our plans without alarming two stalwart men, when she lets out a yell.

"Look! Here comes Rocky."

He's easy to spot because he towers above the crowd. I can't guess what happened by studying his face because he's wearing the inscrutable look that once made us think he wanted to kill us (back during the Bubbles Caper).

Judging by the way he's hurrying, he has either caught a killer or can't wait to get back to Lovie. I'm hoping for both.

Chapter 18

Winners, Losers, and Vanishing Bertha

Lovie grabs Rocky's arm. "Has somebody been killed? What happened?"

Champ goes into hero mode, putting his arm around me and turning so I'm nearest the vendor and he's the one buffeted by the crowd. Obviously he has followed the news about the Elvis murders, but I'll bet he had no idea he'd end up in the middle of it.

"Nobody's dead," Rocky says. "It was a purse snatching. The police nabbed a teenaged girl."

"I'd have sworn it was Bertha." Lovie passes two hot dogs to him.

"I don't think she'd come back here." Champ speaks with a quiet authority that commands attention. "Cody Lacey said Bertha was wanted for questioning in the impersonator murders and that she'd skipped town."

As if Lovie and I don't know. I come in a New York minute of blurting out *Bertha's headed to Las Vegas,* but unless WTVA's anchor, Cody Lacey, said that on the six o'clock news I'd be revealing more than I want on my first post-Jack date.

Not that this is really a date. More like a trial run. I just hope the formidable Miss Lacey didn't blab that I'd been spotted all over town asking about Bertha.

"Did she interview anybody besides the police?" Imagining what the mind-boggling Eric Miller might say, I lose interest in my hot dog.

"Yes." I'm going to hyperventilate. When Champ says, "She did some on-site interviews of festival goers, but nobody wanted to talk about the murder," I can breathe again.

"What did they talk about?" I ask.

"Who was going to win the impersonator contest. Most of them thought Thaxton Miller would win, but since he's also missing they're betting on Terry Matthews."

G. I. Elvis. Who is also a chemist. *Holy cow.*

"Lovie, quick." I grab her arm. Fortunately she has the good sense and the moxie to flash her winning smile at Champ and Rocky.

"Would you excuse us, please," she says. "It's a girl thing."

We hustle back to the Porta Potti. I just hope the woman who called us Jezebels is not lurking somewhere nearby. Ditto, Cody Lacey with her TV camerman.

Or my latest suspect with a vial of poison.

The gods of women who don't want to get caught are with us, and nobody is at the toilet. Squeezed inside, I tell Lovie, "You'll never guess who's a chemist."

"If you drag me away from Rocky and wedge me

in here one more time, you won't have to guess who's going to be the next victim. Out with it."

"G. I. Elvis. The front runner."

"He'd know how to distill poison from plants."

"Exactly. Which goes back to my early theory that one of the impersonators was knocking off the competition."

"But what about Bertha?"

"Shoot, Lovie. Maybe she's slept with G. I. Elvis, too. Or maybe they don't even know each other. Maybe he's the real killer and she's just a killer in bed."

"Move over."

"What?"

"I have to pee."

"Again? It's just been fifteen minutes."

"I had lemonade."

"So did I."

"Hush up and move before I pee on your shoes," Lovie says, and I do. Carefully. Trying to keep the weight evenly distributed.

"I don't know how we're going to stop him if he tries to kill again." In spite of the fact that I'm packing steel, I don't want to use it on anybody, even to defend myself. Besides, my skills are questionable."

"Maybe he won't. They'll be announcing winners in a few minutes."

"If you don't get off the toilet, we're going to miss it."

"If we do, remember whose bright idea this was in the first place." Lovie reaches behind to flush.

"How else was I going to tell you? We can't whisper in front of Champ and Rocky. It's not polite."

"Polite is not what I'm thinking about with Rocky Malone."

"I know what you're thinking, Lovie. Steam's coming from your ears."

"Then let's get out of here before I set the toilet afire."

Nobody's waiting for us except Champ and Rocky, who are still by the corn dog stand. From the looks of things, they're enjoying each other's company. I can picture a future with the four of us sitting around the Thanksgiving table surrounded by little Valentine/Malone and Valentine/Champion offspring in high chairs.

Of course, that's assuming Jack ever gives me a divorce. And that Champ ever wants to see me again after I've dragged him into the center of a homicide investigation.

Not that you'd call Lovie and me detectives. More like accidental investigators. And unlicensed. Okay, and really, really amateur.

I hook my arm through Champ's while he smiles and pats my hand. It's not over-the-moon joy to see me, but it's a start.

The four of us try to press toward the stage to see

Mayor Getty announce the winner of the imper-sonator contest, but the crowd is too thick.

I suggest we go over to the refreshment booth. "It won't be so crowded," I add, "and we can still hear."

"Great idea," Lovie says. "We can have some of my chocolate cherry cake. If it hasn't all been sold."

Frankly, I could use a chocolate stress cure. Between a new suspect popping up and Champ looking better by the minute but still falling short of Jack on the *yes, yes, YES* scale, I'm a bundle of frayed nerves.

It takes a while before we can find out about the cake because the fan club's top three officers are embroiled in a heated argument over camellias, of all things.

"I still say they do better on the north." Tewanda's so mad her corkscrew curls are quiv-ering, and Clytee's red face says that she's not far behind.

"Tewanda's right," Clytee says. "They won't bloom if the morning sun hits them when the dew is on."

Leaned back in the camp chair fanning, her huge patent leather purse at her swollen feet, Beulah Jane looks like a sweet little grandmother. But there's nothing grandmotherly about the way she slaps her fan onto the counter and says, "That's a bald-faced lie."

"Might I remind you that Tewanda and I are officers in the garden club and you are not," Clytee says.

The *garden club*. Why didn't I think of that before? These women know their plants. Which means they know their plant poisons.

I poke Lovie in the ribs, but she gives me this look that clearly says I've lost my tiny mind. She's probably right. Why would sweet little old ladies want to knock off Elvises?

Well, maybe they're not so sweet, but arguing over how to grow camellias is a far cry from poisoning impersonators. Besides, they have no motive.

All this running around in circles is giving me a headache. I rub a forefinger across my temple.

"Are you okay?" Champ says, which means he's very observant and not an easy man to fool. Like Jack.

Am I doomed to repeat my past mistakes? I'd better slow down on the family Thanksgiving/high chair/baby bib thinking.

"I'm great."

The officers finally notice us and look up chagrined, while I stand there with my left eye twitching. Thank goodness, Champ doesn't know my telltale body signals of prevarication.

"Oh, my, my," says Clytee, while Tewanda offers us cake and Beulah Jane urges us to have some peach tea.

I'm grateful for both, as well as the chance to step out of the flow of human traffic and catch my breath.

Over on stage one the microphone roars and Mayor Getty says, "Testing, one, two, three."

Though I can't hear her, I imagine Junie Mae's grabbing her husband's coattails and telling him in her loud stage whisper, "It's working, hon." She's done it at so many public functions, folks around town have adopted *it's working, hon* as the standard response to almost any question, including *do you like the cheese grits*?

"And now, the moment you've all been waiting for." The mayor is yelling into the microphone, which starts roaring again almost drowning out the drumroll and trumpet fanfare. (Listen, I know it's over the top, but southerners enjoy drama and take every opportunity to create one.)

"The winner of this year's Elvis impersonator competition is . . ." Mayor Getty pauses, drawing out the suspense. Beulah Jane, Clytee, and Tewanda clasp hands and wait as if they expect to be raptured.

"Terry Matthews, G. I. Elvis from Pensacola!"

Clytee faints while Tewanda and Beulah Jane jump around squealing. When the new champion of Elvis impersonators takes the microphone and croons "America," they burst into tears of joy.

They don't notice their fallen friend till Rocky lifts Clytee into a chair. Lovie squats beside him with a wet paper napkin and starts rubbing Clytee's pale face while Champ takes her wrist to check her pulse.

"Is she dead?" Beulah Jane's question is matter-of-fact. I guess you get that way about death when you grow old. Or is Beulah Jane still mad at Clytee about the camellias?

"She's just overcome," Tewanda says, but I'm still waiting for the official verdict, never mind that the doctor usually checks dogs and cats. "Terry Matthews is Clytee's nephew," she adds.

Holy cow. G. I. Elvis just jumped to the top of my suspect list, with his aunt Clytee as an accomplice. He has knowledge of poisons, she had access to the food and drink, and they both had motive.

"I was pulling for him," Beulah Jane says. "He's the spitting image of Elvis. I think the King would be pleased."

She pours herself a glass of peach tea, ignoring the rest of us. It's not like her to forget her manners. Judging by her faraway look, I'd say she's in a mild state of shock.

Clytee's eyelids flutter as she comes back to life.

"What happened?" she asks.

"You had a little fainting spell." Tewanda hands her a glass of tea. "Are you all right, hon?"

"Terry won, didn't he?"

As if he heard his cue, the new King of impersonators strolls into the refreshment booth to embrace his aunt while Tewanda and Beulah Jane press around him vying for attention.

It's getting too crowded in here, and besides, I don't like the vibes I'm picking up. Something is amiss; I just don't know what it is. I glance to see if Lovie feels the bad energy, too, but she's so engrossed in Rocky she doesn't even notice me.

I'd herd her back to the Porta Potti for a private discussion, but I don't have the heart. This is Rocky's last night in Tupelo, and unless Lovie flies to his dig in Mexico, she won't see him for a long time. She deserves a night free of everything except the possibility of love.

The four of us bid good-bye to G. I. Elvis and his adoring geriatric fan club, but I don't think any of them hear us.

As we head back into the crowd Lovie says, "I'm ready to call it a day," and Rocky agrees with the speed of a man eager to be alone.

I hug them both good-bye and tell Lovie, "Call me tomorrow."

With the festival over and Clytee's nephew the newly crowned King, she's not likely to strike again. Tomorrow is soon enough to find out if she has the moxie for murder.

Elvis' Opinion #10 on Illegal Holes, Pissants, and Love Triangles

When I hear Jack's Harley, I know I'm caught red-pawed. I could have fooled Callie into thinking digging a hole under the fence was all Hoyt's idea, but my human daddy is going to take one look at my guilty mug and know I was the one who put him up to it. Furthermore, he's going to know why.

It takes one to know one. Jack's a man of the world and I'm a dog-about-town. As much as I enjoy guiding Callie in her journey through life, occasionally I have to have the diversion of some good canine companionship (emphasis on *good,* meaning cute Frenchie and not stupid spaniel).

As a last-ditch effort to cover my crime, I toss my marrow bone into the hole and say, "Quick, Hoyt, act like you're burying it." But he keeps digging so hard you'd think he was trying to find China. That silly dog has a one-track mind.

When the Harley's motor dies (Jack's tucked it in the garage, I see, trying to surprise Callie) I amble over to the gazebo trying to act like I'm out for a midnight stroll in the moonlight.

"Looks like you got into trouble without me." Jack squats to examine my paw, and for a minute I think the sympathy vote (my bandage) is going to get me out of trouble. "You wouldn't know anything about that hole under the fence, would you?"

I howl a few bars of "Ain't Misbehavin'." Although Fats Domino could bring the house down with his rendition, I don't make a dent in Jack.

He gets a shovel from the garage, fills up the hole, then cleans the dirt off us with a water hose and a doggie towel. (*My towel,* thank you very much. I allow Hoyt to use it only because I'm feeling magnanimous tonight.) My human daddy marches us inside and straight to bed, then turns off the light.

"Stay put." Hoyt immediately starts snoring, but I open one eye as Jack heads for the bedroom door. "I mean that, Elvis. Callie will be home soon and I won't have her worrying."

I don't have to ask how he knows. Where Callie's concerned, he has built-in radar. And if that fails, all he has to do is call Charlie. Those two are thicker than pissants at a picnic.

As for staying put, who does he think he's dealing with? Some cheap imitation in an ill-fitting sequined jumpsuit? I'm the real thing, and I'm not about to loll around on my doggie pillow and miss my cues and curtain calls.

Jack heads to the front porch, but I don't trot along behind and get caught. I lie low on my pillow, knowing that I have the advantage. Listen, my human daddy is formidable but unfortunately his ears match. What he gains in looks he misses in acute hearing.

I hear him tromping around the Angel Garden, checking out the crime scene tape, no doubt, thinking how Callie must hate it and making plans to see that it disappears.

If you've guessed that I think my human daddy walks on water, you'd be right.

Finally the chains on the porch swing creak and I hear the soulful strains of Jack's harmonica. He's a good musician. I like to think it's my influence.

If Hoyt wouldn't make a pest of himself, I'd wake him up to hear this. Jack's music always matches his mood. That he chose my hit "Are You Lonesome Tonight?" instead of "Reconsider Baby," by Lowell Fulson or "Walking the Blues" by Willie Dixon says it all.

I'm not just King of the world, I'm king of this hill, and Hoyt might as well learn to genuflect.

In the distance I hear the low-pitched roar of Callie's big Hemi engine. The music stops, which means Jack hears it, too.

I wonder if he also hears that sports car turning onto our road. Easing off my pillow, I pad toward the front and position myself at the window with full view as Callie's headlights hit the driveway. Not far behind is the Ford Mustang convertible I recognize from my unfortunate venture up Highway 371.

The engines cut off and Callie and the doc stroll toward the front steps, hand in hand. I glance at the swing expecting Jack to catapult off the porch and beat the tar out of Luke Champion. But he has blended himself into the dark like a big black panther. (By the way, that's his code name, but you're not getting another word about Jack's profession out of me).

The doc says, "Callie, thank you for a lovely evening," and she tells him, "You're welcome" in her sweet southern drawl that would melt the heart of Hitler.

The aura I'm picking up from the swing is dark enough to start World War III. I brace myself for battle. If Callie invites Champ in, I'll be the only one to save the situation.

I do my best to send her a telepathic message that Jack's on the porch, but she just stands there, oblivious. My humans have so much to learn I'd be daunted if I were a lesser dog.

Instead I send her another message. *Say good night. Come inside. Now.* But she's just standing there looking like Willie Nelson's "Angel Flying Too Close to the Ground" while Champ closes in. Judging by the aura I'm picking up from him, he's not planning to whistle "Let's Be Friends."

He lacks the finesse I used with Ann-Margret. You'd expect more from a man who is around animals all day. As for Callie, without the highly refined senses of a French poodle, she doesn't even notice that Champ could use some lessons on the art of courtship.

He's going to kiss her. I can smell his intent.

With the other third of the love triangle crouched in the swing, this is not going to be pretty.

I'm about to head out the doggie door to rescue the situation when the black panther springs.

"Hello, Cal." Jack's off the porch and planted between them so fast I'm probably the only one who saw him move. "I don't believe we've met." Extending his hand, he says, "Jack Jones. Callie's husband."

"Ex," she says.

"Not quite."

"Soon."

"Never."

"In your dreams." Callie rarely loses her temper, but she's spitting mad.

Champ's just standing by looking like he doesn't know whether to intervene, mind his own business, or turn tail and run. If I don't do something fast, this business is liable to get out of hand.

Drat the bandage and full speed ahead!

I race through the doggie door into the backyard, but the fence keeps me from going around front where all the action is. Being the talented dog I am—and cagey, to boot—I let loose with a mournful rendition of my hit "Peace in the Valley."

It's not perfect for the occasion, but gospel is always good for sympathy and the song fits. If I don't restore some peace between my human parents, I'm liable to end up with Champ's spiteful Persian in the family. It's bad enough to have seven newly adopted stray cats in the family without adding a hateful step-cat.

Callie and Jack come running, just as I knew they would, with Champ matching them step for step. First through the gate, Callie scoops me up and starts crying into my fur.

If I weren't so pleased with myself for putting an end to that pissing contest in my front yard, I'd get down and wallop the daylights out of those two studs. I'll think of a way to get even later. Nobody makes my human mom cry and escapes my wrath.

After Champ checks my bandage to see if everything is all right, he bids Callie a hasty good night and heads his Mustang back to Mantachie. I can tell by the way Jack's looking at me that he knows I'm responsible for getting rid of his competition.

Even more to the point, he's grateful, which means tonight's shenanigans will earn me a good T-bone steak reward.

I rethink my position on revenge. Maybe I won't go whole hog with Jack. Maybe I'll just pull a little stunt or two that will let him know who's in charge around here.

I'm not a dog you want to mess with.

Chapter 19

Complications, Tangled Webs, and Geriatric Courtship

This has turned into the longest, most traumatic day of my life. I'm going to sleep for a year if I ever get to bed. And I can guarantee you, it will be without Jack.

He winces when he puts Elvis back on his guitar shaped pillow. My first instinct is to rush over, ask if he's all right, urge him into an easy chair, then bring a cool cloth for his head and a steaming cup of green tea chai for his soul.

I know, *I know.* I can't make any progress by moving backward.

Still, keeping my distance from Jack is the hardest thing I've done today. Change is so difficult it takes enormous courage and resilience to pull it off. I'm not quite there yet, but I'm working on it.

Elvis immediately falls asleep and I'm left standing by a bed that suddenly takes up all the space in this room while my almost-ex watches me. I bite my lower lip to keep it from trembling.

"I'm very tired, Jack. It's been a long day."

Two steps and he's beside me, cupping my face in his warm hands.

Just don't let him kiss me, that's all I ask.

"Cal." He rubs his thumbs down my damp cheeks. "I'm sorry I made you cry."

Without another word, he exits.

I don't think my legs are going to hold me up more than two more minutes. I let my clothes fall to the floor and climb into bed without hanging them up, without even taking a bath. Pulling the sheets over my dusty feet and up to my chin, I stare at the moonlight pouring through the skylight, and I don't allow myself to think about anything.

Not one single thing.

I wake up to the smell of coffee and the glorious feeling that this is Sunday morning. No hair appointments. No festival. No bodies waiting at Eternal Rest for my magic touch (I hope). Nothing to do but go to Wildwood, the little white clapboard church built on property donated by my grandfather Valentine and filled with stained glass windows in memory of my dearly departed Valentine ancestors.

Well, actually I do have something to do, but I don't intend to check out my latest suspect until I've paid proper homage to the universe and this day. Clytee Estes can wait.

I believe in keeping your priorities straight.

Elvis is stirring, which means if I don't get out of bed soon, he'll drag his doggie dish into the bedroom and let it clank to the floor. Besides, the rich smell of coffee is impossible to resist.

I don't remember setting the timer, but I guess I did. The minute my feet touch the floor, I revise my guess. My clothes are not there. Ditto, my shoes. Which means somebody picked them up and put them in their proper place. It doesn't take a Philadelphia lawyer to figure out who that somebody is.

Jack, of course. Who else has the key to my house and comes and goes as he pleases?

Grabbing my robe, I head to the kitchen. Lo and behold, there's a cheese Danish muffin on my blue lacquered tray along with a Gertrude Jekyll rose. I am grateful and even feel a bit pampered, never mind that the rose is probably from my garden and the cheese Danish is still wrapped in plastic.

I pour myself a cup of coffee and take my breakfast onto the front porch expecting to enjoy it in the swing. But another miracle is waiting for me outside. The crime tape around my Angel Garden has vanished.

I'm so grateful I take my cell phone out of my robe pocket and call to ask Jack about his gunshot wound.

"I'll live," he says, which makes me want to shake him.

"You got shot, Jack. How can you be nonchalant about somebody trying to kill you?"

"What about you, Cal? Who's trying to kill you?"

Bound for him to turn the tables. "Nobody," I tell him.

"That's not what I heard."

Nobody knows about that threatening note except Lovie, and I know she wouldn't tell him. But then, Jack doesn't need anybody to tell him anything. Obviously, he has spies or has bugged everything I own and every place I go. I wonder if there's a law against that.

Still, it seems querulous to pick a fight after the lovely coffee and Danish, especially on Sunday.

"Thank you for breakfast, Jack."

"You're welcome, Cal."

"And for making the crime scene tape disappear."

He doesn't deny it, just says, "My pleasure."

When he tells me good-bye and hangs up without turning this conversation into something for his advantage, I wonder if he's coming down with a fever.

I don't have long to stew over it, though, because Mama calls to invite me to lunch after church. The frame of mind I'm in, her invitation makes me wonder what she's done now. Probably some misdeed that would make me lose sleep.

The first thing I do when I get to church is check out Mama's chin for beard burn. It's either not there or she has cleverly disguised it with makeup.

"What are you staring at?" she asks.

"Nothing. Did you and Fayrene and What's His Name have a good time last night?"

"His name is Thomas and he's coming to lunch. I expect you to behave."

With that, Mama flounces to the organ and starts playing the prelude too loud—"Rescue the Perishing." I wonder if she's trying to tell me something. From where I sit, it looks like all the Valentines are going to perish if things don't change around here soon.

The only good thing I can say about Mama's gentleman friend coming to lunch is that he can't stay long. Philestine Barber's funeral is this afternoon at two, and Mama has to provide the music.

The big surprise at lunch is not Thomas Whitenton (more about him later), but Lovie and Uncle Charlie. He's not here; she is.

Now what? Mama's never had a Sunday lunch without inviting Uncle Charlie. Did he stay away because she didn't invite him or because of Mr. Whitenton?

And Lovie was supposed to be bidding farewell to Rocky instead of sitting at Mama's dining room table eating roast beef, fried okra, and corn on the cob. The first chance I get, I drag her into Mama's bathroom to ask what happened.

"Nothing," is her answer.

The way she's snapping my head off I can guess what that means.

"You mean absolutely nothing, Lovie, or just not what you wanted to happen?"

"Oh, quit pussyfooting around. Rocky didn't find the holy grail. He didn't even look at the map." She applies a fresh coat of red to her lips in spite of the fact we haven't had dessert and Mama's serving apple pie à la mode, which will smear her lipstick. "I must be losing my touch."

"You didn't let him know how miffed you are, did you?"

"What if I did?"

"He might not come back."

"Maybe I don't want him to."

I can tell by Lovie's face she's bluffing. I just hope Rocky didn't leave feeling that she doesn't want him to come back.

Maybe I ought to call him and smooth things over. Since I have Lovie's best interests at heart, I don't see how you could call it meddling.

"What about you? Did Champ kiss you?"

"Sort of, but Jack spoiled it."

"What does that mean?"

I'm fixing to tell when Mama knocks and calls through the door, "The pie's hot and it's rude to tell secrets I can't hear."

We hustle back to the table and listen to Thomas calling Mama "Miss Ruby" and bragging on her cooking, a surefire way to win most women. What he doesn't know is that Mama is not like most women. If he wants to win the heart of Ruby Nell Valentine he's going to have to brag on something besides her cooking. Her hair, for instance, which she has had me dye every color in the rainbow. Or her art. Mama prides herself on her bohemian tastes.

When she went with me to a hair show in New York two summers ago, she bought a huge poster of a nude by Modigliani at the Metropolitan Museum of Art. The poster now lords over the entire back wall of the dining room. It caused quite a stir when she first brought it home, but in spite of Fayrene's advice to drape a cloth over it when the preacher comes to visit, Mama held firm.

"My house is my throne," she said, "and I refuse to abdicate."

I don't intend to let Thomas in on Mama's little vanities. If he flounders around long enough, she'll throw him back for something better.

For one thing, his nose is too long. For another, his purple shirt makes his face look mottled and doesn't match a thing he's wearing. Even worse, he snorts.

This is good pie, snort, snort. What are you doing this afternoon, Miss Ruby, snort?

The only good thing I can say about him is that he has the good sense to leave right after dessert so Mama won't be late for poor old Philistine's funeral.

When I get her alone in the kitchen (except for Lovie, of course), I know better than to come right out and ask whether she invited Uncle Charlie. Back Mama into a corner and she grabs a pole and vaults through the ceiling.

253

"Mama, can you and Uncle Charlie handle everything at the funeral?"

"I'm fine." While I'm covering the pie, she slaps a dish cloth over her shoulder and marches toward the table for the dirty dishes. "If you want to know what Charlie thinks, you'll have to ask him yourself."

"Daddy's fine without us. I already checked."

"Good, Lovie," I say. "I need your help this afternoon." I dither over the pie. "Uncle Charlie loves your apple pie, Mama. Why don't I cut a slice and send it to the funeral home?" Mama acts like she doesn't hear me. "Mama? I said—"

"I heard what you said. If Charlie wants pie, he can come and get it."

I roll my eyes at Lovie, but she just shakes her head. She doesn't worry over Mama and Uncle Charlie the way I do. Or maybe she worries, but covers it so well nobody can tell. A real art, if you ask me.

Chapter 20

Peach Tea, Poison, and Surprising Suspects

When Mama leaves for Eternal Rest, Lovie and I head to my house. While I check on the animals, I tell my cousin the plan.

"I think we can end this murder investigation today. We'll pay a little surprise visit to the fan club's top three officers and see what we can dig up on Clytee Estes."

"I'm in no mood to find out why little old ladies would commit murder. I can't even find Rocky's libido."

"Forget about Rocky's libido. You could be going to jail."

"That's the only reason I'll spend my Sunday afternoon sitting in a parlor full of cats."

"What's wrong with cats?"

"I'm not talking about your cats, Callie. Just cats in general."

Elvis sashays up and licks Lovie's ankles. I swear, I think he understands every word we say. After I tell the animals goodbye, have fun while I'm gone, I get the phone book to look up addresses.

"Why do we need all three?" Lovie says. "Let's just get a confession from Clytee and be done with it."

"How do you propose to do that?"

"The same way I did that purse-snatching twerp in Las Vegas. I'll sit on her."

"Let's hope you don't have to. She's the size of a bird. What harm can she do?"

"You're forgetting she's killed three grown men."

Maybe. I strap on my gun, just in case. When we climb into my Dodge I feel like a woman capable of felling hardened criminals. The Hemi engine roars and we head south on Highway 371.

Clytee Estes lives in a small brick house on Planterville Road. You wouldn't pay it the least bit of attention if it weren't for her yard. In spite of the killing summer heat and three straight years of near drought, her gardens are abloom with so many varieties of plants even I'm pressed to name them all.

Lovie and I bail out, then just stand there gaping at the profusion of scent and color. I wonder if any poison milk vetch or lethal tansy lurks among the innocent beauty.

Clytee comes to the door shading her eyes and squinting. When she recognizes us, she hops down the steps with a spryness thirty-year-olds would envy.

"Law me, I said to myself, who could that be? And it's you!" She takes our hands and her smile is so genuine I decide she's either the best actress in the world or I'm mistaken about her being the killer.

"I hope you don't mind that we just dropped by."

"Goodness, no. Come on in."

We follow her into a living room awash in cat fur. As the mother of seven newly named cats, I'll have to take measures to ensure that this does not happen to my house. Lovie's lips start to curl and I punch her.

"I was just having a little sip of peach tea. Here, have some." Clytee pours an extra glass and hands it to Lovie.

She's got the glass lifted to her lips when I get a flashback of Clytee dispensing peach tea on the tour bus—right before the first impersonator bit the dust.

"No!" I shout and Lovie spills tea all over Clytee's carpet. I poke her in the ribs, just in case she didn't get the picture, but she's turned white as a moon flower. Which means Lovie's on to Clytee.

"I'm so sorry," I tell Clytee. "If you'll get a cloth, I'll wipe it up."

When she heads to the kitchen I whisper to Lovie, "It was the peach tea." I'm sure of it. Every chance they got, the officers of the fan club were passing out peach tea to the impersonators.

We don't have time to speculate further because Clytee's back with a cloth. Though she says she'll wipe the spill, I insist, then get on my knees to repair the damage.

"We dropped by to thank you for the splendid

job you did at the refreshment booth." Flattery usually works. "You were wonderful."

"Oh, I loved every minute it of, Callie. Especially since my nephew won."

"How is he?" I don't know what to do with the damp cloth, so I just fold it up and hold it on my lap while I sit on the sofa.

"On cloud nine, as you can imagine. I wanted him to spend some time with me, but he had to get back to Pensacola."

Lovie and I exchange a look that says *on the lam*. Naturally you wouldn't want to stick around after knocking off your competition.

"He's choir director at his church, you know. Such a fine boy. Last year he was voted Citizen of the Year."

There goes my latest theory. I don't think choir directors will kill you, though I've known a few first sopranos who might disagree with me. I glance at Lovie, who looks like she's about to say a word that will give Clytee a stroke.

"Callie, are you sure you girls don't want some tea? Both of you look a mite peaked."

"We don't have time." I glance at Lovie for some help.

"No, we don't, but it's great tea. I had some at the festival. Could I have the recipe?"

"Oh, it's not mine. It's Tewanda's."

Tewanda was on that bus, too, dispensing tea like it was going out of style tomorrow. But if she put poison in the tea the first day, why didn't all three impersonators die at one time?

I ask if Tewanda made all the tea for the festival, but even if she did, what was her motive for killing impersonators?

"Oh yes. She made all the tea. Her secret is fresh peaches."

What other secret does Tewanda have? Or was the culprit Clytee?

Just as Clytee reaches to set her empty glass on a coaster beside her chair, a big gray Persian leaps into her lap, knocking the tea and a framed photo onto the floor.

"Oh no," she wails. "Elvis."

Elvis? What's going on here?

Clytee and her cat are tangled in the chair and tea is running all over the floor. I leap to rescue the glass with my handy rag while Lovie scoops up the photograph.

Clytee dissolves into tears. "I'll just die if anything happens to that picture. It's the only one I have of Elvis and me."

Lovie turns the picture over. It's a group of children posing on the schoolhouse steps under the caption LAWHON ELEMENTARY SCHOOL, THIRD GRADE.

Elvis is easy to spot. Pictures of the serious looking child wearing overalls and glasses have been widely published.

Clytee pushes the cat off her lap and leans over

259

to point out a pigtailed girl in a checked gingham dress. "That's me." Her finger moves to a chubby, dark-haired girl. "And that's Tewanda."

"Both of you were Elvis' classmates at Lawhon?" I'm not surprised. She would be the right age. In fact, I vaguely recall her name being mentioned in the newspaper a couple of years ago when an enterprising reporter interviewed some of Elvis' classmates.

"Yes."

"Is Beulah Jane on here, too?"

"No. She didn't meet Elvis till later."

"When?" Lovie asks.

"At Milam. She claims they were school sweethearts, but these days every old lady in the fan club claims to be Elvis' girlfriend."

Remembering the dispute between Beulah Jane and Clytee, I don't know what to believe. Was the argument simply over camellias or were there deeper motives? Jealousy over who had the closest relationship with Elvis?

"The nice thing about failing memory," Clytee adds, "is being able to invent an exciting past and really believe it."

She puts the cherished photograph back on the table, and I ask if she can give us a tour of her gardens before we go.

It's ten degrees hotter than when we first arrived, and Clytee's long-winded tour adds to the problem. Sweat is rolling down my face, and if my clothes get any damper Clytee will see the imprint of my gun.

I punch Lovie and she blurts out, "Do you grow poison plants?"

Clytee moves so fast she could win the senior Olympic races. Perched in front of Lovie like a ruffled-up sparrow, she shakes her bony finger under my cousin's nose.

"Young lady, if you think I'd grow oleander and risk Terry's precious children getting poisoned, you ought to be spanked. I would never do such a thing. And I can't believe you'd accuse me."

"Oh no, Lovie didn't mean to accuse you. She's been studying herbs lately." I invent as I talk, but Clytee is not convinced. "For her catering business, you know. She's just trying to learn from an expert gardener. That's all."

Flattery does the trick. "You're a good girl, Callie." Clytee smiles, but only at me, while Lovie stomps off to my truck.

"I'm really sorry if we upset you, Clytee."

"That's all right, dear." She pats my hand. "I know *you* didn't mean any harm. If your cousin really wants to know about poison plants, ask Tewanda. She's the one who grows them."

I join Lovie in my Dodge and we head toward Tewanda's house. "I don't think Clytee's the killer, Lovie."

"I think we're wasting our time. These little old

ladies are just growing flowers and trying to one-up each other about who was closer to their idol."

"I still say we need to check them all out."

"Besides, if Clytee was going to knock off her nephew's competition, why did she pick the three worst singers?"

Lovie should know. She was training to be a professional musician before her mother died.

"Maybe she's tone-deaf," I say. "Or maybe he selected the victims for reasons we don't know yet."

Lovie turns up the air-conditioning, then starts fanning with the Wildwood church bulletin I left on the seat.

"If we're going to catch the right person this time, it's going to take more than sitting in some little old lady's parlor on Sunday afternoon discussing flowers."

"What do you suggest? False mustaches and felt fedoras? Good grief, Lovie. Tewanda and Beulah Jane know us. They'd see right through disguises."

"You talk about flowers if you want to. I'm doing some real detective work."

Translated: snooping. I'm better at it than Lovie, but I'll go along with her scheme. She needs something to occupy her mind besides her failure to find Rocky's libido.

Tewanda lives in a small pink stucco house with a circular drive in east Tupelo, not far from Elvis' birthplace. As I enter the drive from the east side, Tewanda roars out the west.

I watch her Honda Civic disappear in the direction of Barnes Crossing Mall. "Clytee called to tell her about our visit."

"Who made you Houdini?" Lovie's not in a good mood (with cause, I'll grant you). I have reasons to be surly, too (both of them male), but I pride myself on holding up under pressure.

"Clytee was in Reed's Bookstore the day you asked about poison plants, and somebody put the threatening note on my pickup that day. If Clytee didn't do it, she spread the word to Tewanda and Beulah Jane, and one of them did. It's obvious, Lovie."

"Well, get the lead out and let's get this over with."

Lovie always talks about my driving. I'd make a remark she wouldn't like, but it's Sunday.

As we head toward Beulah Jane's I have a strong feeling she won't be home, either, and it turns out I'm right. Breaking and entering is not an option because it's broad daylight and people are sitting on their front porches hoping to see something worth talking about.

Stymied, we head to Eternal Rest to see what Mama and Uncle Charlie are up to.

In his case, reading, and in Mama's, no good.

While Lovie's in the office talking to Uncle Charlie, I head to the kitchen and find Mama in a huddle with Bobby Huckabee.

"Mama, did I hear you mention a séance at Fayrene's?"

She and Bobby jump like the guilty. "How do I know what you heard?" she says. "I'm no mind reader."

"But I am."

"Hush, Bobby." Mama gets up and pours me a glass of Prohibition Punch, the Valentine family remedy for everything from a broken heart to a broken fingernail. "You look like you could use this. Sit down." She motions me to a chair. "How's Jack? I talked to him and he didn't sound too perky."

Naturally they talked. They have a mutual admiration society. Where he's concerned, Mama seizes every opportunity to meddle.

Ignoring her question, I sit at the table, grateful the punch has plenty of vodka. No sooner am I in my chair than Bobby says, "I see danger from a dark-eyed stranger."

"Not now, Bobby." Mama pats my hand. "Now tell me what's going on with you and that sweet man."

"Mama, I can think of many ways to describe Jack Jones, but sweet is not one of them." I take a fortifying sip of punch. "Has anybody heard from Bertha?"

"No. The law is still looking for her."

"What's Uncle Charlie going to do with poor old dead Dick?"

"You'll have to ask Charlie."

"Mama, whatever's eating you two, I wish you'd fix it."

"Have some more punch." She refills my cup and quite frankly, I'm glad to let her. Lovie can drive. When I get home I plan to do nothing but curl up on the sofa with Elvis and take a nap.

My phone rings and I answer it out of pure habit. When I hear a male "hello" I wish I'd checked the caller ID first. Today I don't need one more added complication.

"Elvis is lonely," Jack says.

"What are you doing in my house?"

"I'm taking him for a while."

"Wait a minute," I say, but he has already hung up. I reach for another cup of Prohibition comfort.

Lovie joins us in the kitchen and pours herself a cup.

"Just drink one, Lovie. I'm on my third. You're driving."

"In that case." She fills a plastic pitcher of punch. "We'll go by my house for clothes. I'm staying with you tonight."

"It works for me."

I don't want to be alone, either. In addition to kidnapping my dog, Jack's probably planning to waylay me tonight, and I'm fresh out of willpower.

Leaving Uncle Charlie holed up in his apartments above the funeral home and Mama holed up in the kitchen with Bobby Huckabee, we step into the parking lot and a blast of heat. I'm just getting ready to ask Lovie if she knows what Mama and Bobby are plotting when she says, "What's that on your windshield?"

It's another note. I pluck it off and she reads it aloud, " 'I hear you've been snooping again. Stay out of my business.' What the devil?"

"Not the devil, Lovie. The killer."

"It must be Clytee."

"Or she's perfectly innocent and it's one of the cronies she called." I fold the note and stick it in my purse.

"Maybe Bertha doubled back." Lovie swivels around looking for trouble, and I do, too.

If one of the three geriatrics fan club officers or Bertha Gerard is back there, I'm pulling out my gun, and I don't much care what I hit as long as I draw blood.

"Let's go, Lovie."

She pulls out of the parking lot and I settle into the passenger side. But I have the eerie feeling somebody is watching.

Elvis' Opinion #11 on Motorcycles, Séances, and Courtship

Jack knows what a dog likes, but he doesn't have a clue about a woman. When I spot him coming up the sidewalk with a wad of wilted wildflowers, I figure he needs some serious counseling on courtship. It'll be up to me.

"Hey, boy," he says, then goes straight to the kitchen and sticks his floral mistake in a Mason jar.

I howl a few lines of "Red Roses for a Blue Lady" (not one of my hits, but it fits the occasion). Jack bends down and scratches my ears.

"You're not feeling good, are you, boy?"

I'd chalk my human daddy off as hopeless in the romance department if I didn't know from some serious voyeurism (listen, I'm not perfect) that he's hot in the sack.

He calls Callie to say he's taking me (another major mistake for a man hoping to win points) and we head off toward Gas, Grits, and Guts.

Free at last. With the wind blowing my ears back I feel like anything is possible. Even a little visit to my own ladylove. If I can catch Jack in the right mood (meaning when he's not mooning over how to win Callie back now that another man is in the picture), maybe I can talk him into a little side trip to see my knocked-up Frenchie and I won't have to fool with getting that silly spaniel to do my dirty work.

Jack helps me off his bad boy's Harley and I sashay into Gas, Grits, and Guts expecting a round of applause from my local admirers and a little smackeral of something good from Jarvetis.

Well, bless'a my soul, what's this I hear? A public debate (to put a polite spin on it) between Mooreville's answer to Lucy and Desi over Bobby Huckabee. And they don't stop when they see us coming, either.

Jarvetis is saying, "Fayrene, for the last time, I will not allow you to expand the break room in my store so Bobby Huckabee can hold séances."

Little does he know—she and Ruby Nell have already drawn up the plans, and Fayrene's already hired a contractor.

"Whose store did you say?" Fayrene owns fifty-one percent of this establishment, a fine point that's landed her hapless spouse into some serious trouble and deprived me of my treat. Jarvetis has more on his mind today than pickled pigs' lips.

"It's not enough that you and Ruby Nell go all over the country flashing your skirts."

"It's called dancing, Jarvetis, and I asked you to go."

"This is the last straw. I'm not ruining the reputation of Gas, Grits, and Guts with devil worshipers."

He stomps to the coffeepot and she flounces to

the back room. I'm surprised she let that devil worship remark pass.

If I don't do something fast, Jarvetis is going to be on the next train to Memphis taking my snacks and my pal Trey, to boot. Besides that, if Gas, Grits, and Guts shuts down, Mooreville's entire social structure will collapse.

But not to worry. I have a plan.

While Jack's over by the canned goods ignoring the proprietors and trying to figure out whether to have Sweet Sue chicken and dumplings or sardines for supper, I mosey out the door and around back where my old pal Trey is lolling under the oak tree enjoying a ham bone. Fresh, from the smell of it.

I lean casually against the kennel fence. Mooreville society is not fixing to collapse while I'm in charge.

"Get your redbony self over here, Trey. We've got some important business to discuss."

Chapter 21

Red Roses, Wilted Daisies, and Jealous Lovers

I'm still feeling jumpy when we get to Lovie's, so I follow her around the house while she throws her stuff into an overnight bag.

You'd never call her a neatnik. Her clothes are scattered all over the house.

So are the roses from Rocky. I try not to think about that, about Lovie having a sweet man but acting like she doesn't because his old-fashioned ideals clash with her need to feel loved. When it comes to love, she has a fast food mentality (wanting everything instantly). I've told her so, but I'm afraid she doesn't hear.

Both of us need some getaway time on the farm. Maybe we'll do that tonight.

"Lovie, have you heard Mama planning a séance?"

"No, but it wouldn't surprise me. Aunt Ruby Nell's wanted to get in touch with Uncle Michael ever since he died."

Why didn't I know that? And once Mama sets her mind, there's no stopping her.

"Good grief, the next thing I know, Mama will be going on television."

"What's so bad about that? If things don't heat

up with Rocky soon, I may have to take out my frustration on the microwaves."

"*Airwaves,* Lovie. You sound like Fayrene."

"No, I meant what I said. I have a new recipe for microwaved fudge brownies."

She goes into her big kitchen with the shiny green tiles and copper pots. It smells of the wonderful herbs drying on a rack, fresh chocolate from her latest creation, and the cinnamon-scented orchid blooming on her windowsill. I want to sit down in here and not move for about three hours. I don't want to meditate, think, listen to music, or even dream. I just want to get into a Zen-like state of being.

She's buried in the pantry rattling cans and bottles.

"What are you doing, Lovie?"

"Getting snacks. You never have any." True, which explains my skinny backside. "I thought we'd go down to the farm tonight."

Sometimes she reads my mind. I believe in mental telepathy one hundred percent. But don't let that fool you into thinking I want Mama trying to contact Daddy just because she thinks Bobby Huckabee's blue eye really is psychic.

"If you can bring me back in the morning, I'll just leave my van here and we'll take your truck."

"Fine." Unless anybody has a big emergency like a wedding or a funeral, I close my beauty shop on Mondays.

Lovie's packed enough to withstand the Civil War siege of Vicksburg and we finally head out the door. While she's locking up, a little car roars out from the curb a block down the street, and I strain my eyes to see the driver. The car is not a Honda Civic, so it can't be Tewanda.

"Lovie, did you notice what kind of car Clytee drives."

"Buick. Why?" She heads toward my Dodge Ram and I follow so close I step on her heels. She says a word and turns around. "What's the matter with you?"

"Somebody's following us."

"If anybody messes with me today they'd better be prepared to lose body parts."

Maybe I ought to give Lovie the gun. We climb into the Dodge and head to Mooreville. Armored with bad attitude, she keeps her eye on the road, but I look over my shoulder all the way home.

When we get to my house I make Lovie go in with me and get a flashlight so we can search all around the grounds. Ordinarily Elvis would be home to keep intruders away, but we all know where he is now. With the enemy.

Okay, so that's not quite fair. Jack is not the enemy, just the man who wants custody of my dog. And who won't give me a divorce. And who pops out of nowhere when I find a man who could take his place.

272

I'm shining my flashlight under the house while Lovie shines hers in the bushes. "There's nothing out here, Callie."

"How can you be sure?"

"Your yowling cats are enough to scare away Jack the Ripper."

I hurry to feed the cats and Hoyt while Lovie goes back inside. Before fall I think I'll build a little cat house with seven cat beds and a warming lamp to keep them cozy this winter. That way they'll be safe and toasty and I won't have to worry about cat hair all over the house. I don't fancy it as a fashion accessory on all my skirts and pants, and Mama's allergic to cat dander.

While I'm at it, I need to get a feeder and teach them to use it before my trip to Italy next summer. Since Jack left, self-sufficiency has been my other major goal. (I'm not even going to get into the primary one, which I break with such regularity it would be depressing if I couldn't blame Jack. He's the one who keeps breaking and entering.)

I tell my cats good night, pet them all around, then go into the house and check my messages. There are three. The first is from Champ asking me out to dinner, a relief considering our shaky start. I call him, get his machine, and leave a message accepting his invitation.

The other two are from Mama telling me I ought to be checking on Jack's health and if I don't some other woman will because he's a catch. Her words, not mine.

Tomorrow is soon enough to tell Mama my marriage is really over (a truth she might as well start accepting). After a good night's sleep and a long, quiet evening I'll feel more like coping with her.

I go into the kitchen, where Lovie is sorting through her stash of snacks. She has already poured two glasses of Prohibition Punch, and brings one straight to me.

"What's with the daises?" she asks.

I spot the flowers on the table. In spite of all common sense and good intentions, I head that way and bury my face in the petals. I don't know where Jack got them—probably plucked from some neighbor's yard because mine doesn't have daisies. His simple gift melts my resolves and stirs up my eggs.

Jack would make a wonderful father except for one little flaw. He's always trying to get himself killed.

"Is somebody trying to tell us something?" Lovie slugs her punch. "Daisies foreshadow death."

"I think that's lilies, Lovie. Besides, I think we were followed in Tupelo. Even a smart killer can't be two places at the same time." I take another sip of punch. "Unless he had an accomplice."

"I don't want to think about any of that. Grab a quilt and let's go. I'll get the food and drink."

I don't want to think about murder, either.

Anyhow, I'm feeling a little light-headed and the room is beginning to look fuzzy.

It will be a bit cooler on the farm by the lake, and the fresh air will clear my head.

Besides, there's a full moon out tonight. Problems have a way of fading in the moonlight. Throw in a sky full of stars, and if you're the kind of woman who is awed by the splendor of the universe (which I am), your problems will downright disappear.

Though I'm just starting to teach myself a few chords, I grab my guitar. Music and moonlight soothe the soul in a way that all the Sunday sermons in the South cannot.

"Are you about ready?" Lovie's calling from the front room.

"Just a minute."

I've remembered my gun. There's no way I'm heading off for an evening of relaxation with a weapon strapped to my thigh.

I unbuckle the holster strap, toss the whole thing in the top dresser drawer, then strip off my skirt, put on a comfortable pair of jeans, and slip into my favorite Steve Madden moccasins.

My cell phone rings but I remember to look at the caller ID. It's Jack. As much as I'm tempted, I don't answer.

Nothing is going to spoil my evening.

Chapter 22

Guitars, Moonlight, and Smoking Shotguns

As we head down the road to the farm I notice Mama's car at Gas, Grits, and Guts. My instinct tells me she and Fayrene are up to their ears in trouble.

"Do you want to stop?" Lovie asks.

"No. Keep on driving."

Tonight, their problems are not mine. Let poor old Jarvetis deal with it.

We turn into a lane shaded by a canopy of trees and suddenly we're on the Valentine homestead. It's Mama's now, but when I was growing up it was the gathering place for extended family. They flocked here nearly every Sunday afternoon, and these hills rang with laughter.

My Dodge rattles across the cattle gap (an opening in the fence featuring a series of railroad ties spaced far enough apart that cattle can't cross), and we're on sacred ground. I know that sounds like sacrilege, but every time I set foot on this patch of earth I feel connected to the universe in a way that restores my sense of balance and harmony.

Lovie and I spread the quilt under our favorite oak tree on the hillside that overlooks the lake on

Mama's farm. I'm still limber enough to sit cross-legged, but Lovie is not. She reclines, then starts issuing orders like Cleopatra on her barge.

"Pass the cake and don't spare the punch. While you're at it, toss me one of those cardboard fans. I think I just got a hot flash."

"You're too young, Lovie."

"Don't tell me what I can and cannot do."

I'm glad her good mood is back. Lovie enjoys a good-natured argument, but only when she's feeling relaxed.

I eat two pieces of cake and she eats three; then she pours herself another glass of punch.

"I thought you were driving, Lovie."

"We'll spend the night, like we used to."

Sleeping with stars, we called it. We'd badger Mama or Aunt Minrose or Uncle Charlie until one of them would bundle up quilts and blankets and flashlights and then bring us up here for a night of telling ghost stories and singing.

I pick up my guitar, pluck a few chords, and start singing one of the old hymns Lovie and I grew up with—"Love Lifted Me."

"Sing something else," she says.

"Why? I like that song."

"I do, too, but not tonight."

I segue into "Rock of Ages" and Lovie tells me to cut it out. Rocky is what's eating her, of course.

"Can't you play something besides a hymn?" she says.

"Not much."

Hymns are easy. You can play one with only three chords. If Jack and I have a friendly divorce (if we ever get a divorce), maybe he'll give me guitar lessons.

I try to strike up "On the Road Again," one of Willie Nelson's super hits, to remind Lovie of our trip to Italy next year, but the guitar's not cooperating.

"Something's wrong with your G string, Callie."

"You tend to your G-string, and I'll tend to mine."

If Lovie's just going to sit there giving advice, I might as well quit playing. When I stand up to take the guitar back to my Dodge Ram, a bullet whizzes by my head and blows a hole in the tree.

"Duck, Callie."

Lovie grabs my legs and drags me down just as another shotgun blast knocks down a limb.

"Has that hunter gone crazy?" I'm shaking all over. "He nearly killed me."

"That's no hunter." Lovie's right. It's dark out there, and there's a hole in the tree big enough to drive a Mack truck through. Whoever is shooting at us means business.

"Holy cow." Another blast passes over us so close it parts my hair the wrong way. "What are we going to do, Lovie?"

"Head for the woods. Zigzag."

Lovie and I set out across the dark pasture. Major

278

mistake. Cows have tromped out potholes and left smelly gifts every which way. Lovie stumbles in a hole and goes down.

"Keep going, Callie," she yells, but I'm not about to leave her behind as a target for the crazed killer.

You don't grow up on a farm without knowing a twelve-gauge double-barreled shotgun when you come face-to-face with it. They can shoot a hole in you big enough to loose all major body organs, and I don't intend to be a donor. Not tonight, anyhow.

I grab Lovie's arm and jerk her upright as another blast plows a hole in the ground next to us. Dirt flies all over my shoes.

Now, that makes me mad. What if she'd shot my leg off? I'd never be able to wear Jimmy Choo stilettos again.

I turn around and shake my fist at the source. "You maniac. What's wrong with you?"

"You couldn't stay out of it, could you?" It's a woman's voice, followed by another blast. In the dark with all the shooting and carrying on, I can't tell who it is.

"Who's out there?" I yell.

"Are you crazy?" Lovie jerks me back to the ground. "You're a sitting duck."

"I was standing."

"Smart-ass. You know what I mean."

We lie low, but our stalker is silent. Maybe she's reloading or maybe she's moving to a position to get a better shot. I'm not naive enough to think she's gone home.

"Crawl," Lovie whispers, and we drag belly first out of the dubious protection of the pothole toward the open patch of earth between us and the woods. The friendly moonlight suddenly becomes a spotlight that could send us to an early grave.

Out of the corner of my eye I see a figure running toward the woods. And I think I know who it is.

"Run, Lovie. She's trying to get the drop on us."

We rise up and dash toward the shelter of a stand of cedar trees. They're thicker than the oaks and pines and will offer more protection.

"Did you get a good look?" Lovie whispers.

"Yes. I think it's Beaulah Jane. Shhh. Here she comes."

In a print dress and lace-up shoes, Beulah Jane would look like a little old grandmother lost in the woods except for two things—her shotgun and her hair. The weapon is lethal and her hair is a wild mess. It's covered with leaves and brambles and sticking up from her head like a tower of cotton candy.

"Come out!" she yells. "I know you're in there."

She cocks the gun and pours a blast into the cedar tree next to Lovie. If I don't do something fast, the next shot is liable to go right through her. Or me.

I don't intend to die before I've ever had a chance to add to the Valentine family tree.

"Beulah Jane." I've heard it throws criminals off if you know their name. "You don't want to kill us."

"You set the cops on me."

"We didn't." But I'm glad to hear they're doing their job. I was beginning to think that criminal detection in this town would be left up to Lovie and me. A scary thought.

"Yes, you did. Clytee said you were snooping. You stole my tansy oil and took it to the cops."

So that's the poison. I remember reading that it takes only a few drops of the lethal oil. Within two to four hours the victim convulses and dies. I've even figured out how Beulah Jane did it. While she scurried all over the festival offering peach tea to the impersonators, she reached into her purse to add a little something extra to the ones she wanted to kill.

What I don't know is why.

"We're not armed, Beulah Jane. If you kill us it will be cold-blooded murder." She's quiet, thinking it over, I hope. "I'm sure you didn't mean to kill the impersonators."

"Oh yes, I did. Their singing was sacrilege. The three who died didn't deserve to wear the signature clothing of my sweetheart, let alone try to sing his songs."

Clytee said Beulah Jane claimed to be Elvis' sweetheart, but I never dreamed she'd be taking her role seriously after sixty-something years.

281

"I would have gotten away with it, too, if you and Lovie hadn't stuck your noses into it."

Beulah Jane lifts the shotgun. In the moonlight the steel double barrels look big enough to blow us straight through the Pearly Gates (at least, that's the direction I hope I'm going).

I'm out of breath and out of options. Lovie and I wrap our arms around each other and hold on. It'll all be up to Mama and Uncle Charlie now, and I can guarantee they'll give us a send-off that will be the talk of Mooreville for generations to come.

The last thing I hear is "Drop the gun, Beulah Jane."

When I come to, Uncle Charlie and Lovie are standing over me and Sheriff Trice is leading Beulah Jane toward a squad car.

"What happened?"

"Jack," Uncle Charlie tells us, and that says it all.

In the distance I hear his big Harley roaring down the road, and I'm eternally grateful for two things. He saved my life and he didn't stick around to collect a reward.

Elvis' Opinion #12 on Hideaways, Harleys, and Hot Water

In case you're wondering who cracked the case, that would be yours truly. Jack got a call from Charlie while I was straightening things out at Gas, Grits, and Guts (more about that later), so the two of us took off to Beulah Jane's house. If it hadn't been for me keeping a lookout while Jack went inside, he might never have had time to find the incriminating evidence. After he got the tansy oil, he rounded up the cops and cornered the killer on Ruby Nell's farm.

We got there just in the nick of time, too. Most folks wouldn't look on a bullet to the shoulder as a blessing, but I do. If my human daddy hadn't been shot down in Mexico and come home to discuss this business with Charlie and take care of things, I might have lost my human mom.

And there'd be no living with Jack if he lost Callie.

Listen, he's taking care of her even as I speak. While I'm sitting out here on the Harley in my doggie seat wearing my special helmet and snacking on a pepperoni pizza bribe, he's inside Vanelli's pretending to eat dinner—at a table right next to Champ and Callie. I don't have to see this to know. He told me the plan before we left Magnolia Manor.

He has no intention of letting Champ get his hands on Callie.

Jack probably won't say a thing, just sit there like a brooding mountain and make Luke Champion wish he'd gone out on the town with another woman. Any woman except Jack's.

As for the murder case, Beulah Jane's been indicted and Charlie got a postcard from Bertha today. She and Thaxton got married in the Chapel of Love in Las Vegas. She said he's gaining impersonator fame with nightly appearances in Hot Tips. I doubt that. I know Vegas like the back of my paw, and Hot Tips is not the place to shoot you to stardom.

Bertha also wrote, "Do what you want to with Dick. I'm not coming back."

There's no way Charlie Valentine is going to put that poor sucker in the ground without fanfare. He and Ruby Nell have put aside their differences long enough to plan the unfortunate impersonator's going-away ceremony.

Thanks to Callie, it will be a doozie. She said to them, "Poor dead Dick deserves a jazz funeral complete with a marching band."

I'm considering selling tickets to this one.

Meanwhile, Trey is hiding out down on the farm, and Jarvetis is so busy looking for his best redbone hound he's postponed leaving Fayrene.

My machinations, thank you, thank you very much. All I had to do was jiggle the kennel fence so the latch popped up and Trey could race to freedom.

He knows the plan. I'll see that he gets plenty of food. (Not that he couldn't fend for himself. He can catch a rabbit faster than any hound I know.) He'll stay put till Fayrene gets out of hot water with Jarvetis.

If Ruby Nell keeps turning up the heat, that won't be any time soon. She and Fayrene went right ahead with the séance in spite of Jarvetis claiming it would be over his dead body. Now they're charging forth to build a bigger room.

So they can invite more spirits, I guess.

I don't know why they don't consult me. I'm the reincarnated dog around here. I could get some spirits into Gas, Grits, and Guts that would have the place rocking. Johnny Cash, to name one. All they have to do is ask, and maybe sweeten the request with a few pickled pigs' lips.

Just not tonight.

Callie and Champ are hurrying toward his car, and strolling right behind them is my human daddy. From the looks of his grin, I'd say he accomplished his mission.

Jack straps on his helmet and revs up the motorcycle.

"They're headed to Callie's house for some TV viewing. How does *Three's* Company sound to you, pal?"

Like music to my ears. No way am I going to

stand for a pack of *his, mine,* and *ours* animals. As long as Callie and Jack stay married, I'm top dog, and I plan to keep it that way.

The big Harley roars out of the parking lot and we hit a long stretch of highway. By the time Callie and Champ get to her house, Jack will be sitting on Callie's couch holding the remote. He'll even have the popcorn made. For three. Four, if you count me, and anybody worth his salt does.

I throw back my head and howl a few bars of "Blue Suede Shoes."

Elvis has left the building.

Center Point Publishing
600 Brooks Road ● PO Box 1
Thorndike ME 04986-0001 USA

(207) 568-3717

US & Canada:
1 800 929-9108
www.centerpointlargeprint.com